"I can't look. You do it."

"You sure?"

She just couldn't. "I'm sure."

Closing her eyes, Rachel waited an interminable heartbeat of time, heard David suck in his breath.

"Oh my God." His words were a reverent whisper.

"You're kidding!" She knew he'd never joke about this. Still, maybe he'd misread the test, or… "Let me see."

He moved aside, letting out an earsplitting whoop even as she viewed the proof for herself. "We're pregnant!"

Her knees trembled. She was carrying his baby. Tears welled in her eyes. Before she could classify them as happy crying or something more bittersweet, he pulled her into his strong arms.

And kissed her.

Dear Reader,

In 2007, I created the town of Mistletoe, Georgia, for a Harlequin American Christmas novella and I loved the setting and characters so much that I knew I had to return! (Luckily, my editor agreed.) Many of you wrote to ask if there would be more Mistletoe stories and the answer is a resounding yes: four, as a matter of fact! One for each season.

First up is the winter tale of David and Rachel Waide, a husband and wife who love each other deeply but have lost their way, due in part to the emotional toll of infertility struggles. The last thing they want to do is upset their loved ones at Christmas with news of a separation, especially when David's brother is about to get married. The entire Waide family is busy with wedding preparations. So David and Rachel agree to put on a happy face until the end of December. Amid the magical holiday season and poignant reminders of what matrimony means, can they rediscover what drew them together in the first place and maybe discover brand new gifts as well?

Watch for the next book, *Mistletoe Cinderella*, to be out April 2009! You can learn about all four stories at my Web site, www.TanyaMichaels.com.

Happy reading & enjoy your stay,

Tanya

Mistletoe Baby

TANYA MICHAELS

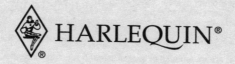

HARLEQUIN®

TORONTO • NEW YORK • LONDON
AMSTERDAM • PARIS • SYDNEY • HAMBURG
STOCKHOLM • ATHENS • TOKYO • MILAN • MADRID
PRAGUE • WARSAW • BUDAPEST • AUCKLAND

ISBN-13: 978-0-373-75239-3
ISBN-10:   0-373-75239-3

MISTLETOE BABY

Copyright © 2008 by Tanya Michna.

www.eHarlequin.com

Printed in U.S.A.

ABOUT THE AUTHOR

Tanya Michaels started telling stories almost as soon
as she could talk...and started stealing her mom's
Harlequin romances less than a decade later. In 2003,
Tanya was thrilled to have her first book, a romantic
comedy, published by Harlequin. Since then, Tanya's
sold nearly twenty books and is a two-time recipient
of the Booksellers' Best Award as well as a finalist for
the Holt Medallion, National Readers' Choice Award
and Romance Writers of America's prestigious RITA®
Award. Tanya lives in Georgia with her husband, two
preschoolers and an unpredictable cat, but you can visit
Tanya online at www.tanyamichaels.com.

Books by Tanya Michaels

HARLEQUIN AMERICAN ROMANCE
1170—TROUBLE IN TENNESSEE
1203—AN UNLIKELY MOMMY
1225—A DAD FOR HER TWINS

HARLEQUIN TEMPTATION
968—HERS FOR THE WEEKEND
986—SHEER DECADENCE
1008—GOING ALL THE WAY

HARLEQUIN NEXT
DATING THE MRS. SMITHS
THE GOOD KIND OF CRAZY
MOTHERHOOD WITHOUT PAROLE

This holiday story about marriage—
one couple preparing to join their lives
while another couple rediscovers their love—is
dedicated to real-life married couple Jane and Eric,
aka The Mims Who Saved Christmas. Thank you so
much for everything you've both done, for always
picking up the phone no matter the hour, for always
having a kitchen stocked full of comfort food, and
for always laughing at the right moments.

Chapter One

It was the worst basketball game in Waide brother history—even including the one when David, at fourteen, had been showing off for a cute neighborhood girl and ended up with stitches. At least he'd sunk the layup before taking the trip to the emergency room, not to mention going on the subsequent movie date and having his first real kiss.

Given David and Tanner's combined performance this December afternoon, however, a team from Whiteberry Elementary could probably take them. David's shots kept going wild. He knew he was throwing with too much force, taking repressed anger out on a ball that had never hurt anyone.

"This is getting humiliating," he called as Tanner jogged after the ball for the rebound.

"Getting?" His younger brother smirked. "Then you haven't been paying attention for the past hour. The irony is how hard you're trying. Last time I saw a guy push himself like that was Dylan Echols when he was up for a baseball scholarship. But you're not a high school athlete, you're a middle-aged store manager."

"Thirty-one is *not* middle age," David retorted. "And it's not like you're doing any better. You couldn't hit the broad side of a barn."

Tanner grinned, unfazed. "Guess my mind's on my beautiful bride-to-be."

David rolled his eyes, but they both knew he was happy for his brother. Ecstatic even. Definitely not jealous.

"So we know my excuse," Tanner continued. "You want to tell me what's eating you?"

No. He and Rachel had agreed not to break the bad news until after the holidays, after the wedding. Maybe by then, it wouldn't even be necessary. Their problems could be nothing more than a temporary aberration brought on by Rachel's medication and mood swings. "Nothing's wrong."

"You sure? I could pay you back for all that great advice you used to give me."

"Great advice you consistently ignored."

Growing up, there'd been an unspoken friction between David—the oldest sibling, high school valedictorian and heir apparent at the family store—and Tanner—the restless rebel who couldn't seem to win their dad's approval. With time and distance, the two brothers had matured and their stern father had mellowed. Last winter, when Tanner had moved back to Mistletoe, family peace had been restored. At the same time, Tanner had rekindled his relationship with high school sweetheart Lilah Baum. On December 28, the two would finally marry.

When his brother didn't start dribbling, David straightened. "We done?"

"Not unless your ego can't take it anymore." Tanner checked his watch. "I need to clean up before I meet Lilah for dinner, but she and the girls should still be at the fitting."

David looked away; one of those "girls" included his wife. Amidst all of Tanner and Lilah's nuptial preparations, David couldn't help being reminded of his own wedding. How excited he'd been, how in love. He'd known from the moment he'd seen Rachel Nietermyer that he wanted to spend the rest of his life with her. He swallowed hard.

"Can I get your opinion on something?" Tanner asked.

Only if it has nothing to do with marriage or women in general. David's own first year of marriage had been blissful. If he could go back now, what advice would he give himself? What could he have done differently? He'd worked to give Rachel everything she needed. Of course, the one thing she'd truly wanted hadn't been within his power.

"I might not be your best bet for wisdom," David said. "Maybe you should talk to Dad or Mom."

Zachariah and Susan Waide were informal experts on relationships; they'd been together nearly forty years. No Waide David knew of had ever been divorced.

Tanner laughed, the carefree sound of a confident man in love. "It's not a huge crisis requiring the big guns. I glanced at one of Lilah's magazines, and some bridal checklists mentioned a wedding present. I'm stymied. We're getting married three days after Christmas. Is she going to expect something even bigger than her Christmas gifts? If I get her something too extravagant and she gets me a small token, am I going to embarrass her?"

"Seriously? These are the things you worry about?"

"Stupid, right?" Lowering his gaze, Tanner bounced the ball against the concrete. "But this is *Lilah*. I've screwed up in the past. She deserves... I want everything to be perfect."

Remembering various anniversaries, Christmases and birthdays, David sighed. "No, it's not stupid." Still, *perfect* was a tall order.

He kept his skepticism to himself. What did he know? Maybe Lilah and Tanner would find their own version of perfect. Perhaps in marriage, the erstwhile prodigal son would succeed where the overachieving problem-solver was currently failing.

RACHEL WAIDE suspected that the best way to survive emotional trauma—separating from your husband, just as a crazy for-instance—was to depend on the support of friends and family. Which was spectacularly unhelpful in her case, since she and David had sworn *not* to tell any of their friends and family. Weddings should be festive, celebratory events, and she and David refused to ruin Tanner and Lilah's moment.

Blinking away the omnipresent threat of tears, she gave her reflection a reprimanding scowl. *Think happy thoughts.* She wasn't going to let herself turn into the self-centered Ebenezer Scrooge of bridesmaids, visited Christmas Eve by three vengeful wedding coordinators.

"Rach?" Lilah's perky voice came from the other side of the thick mauve curtain. "How's the dress look?"

Tight. Rachel dropped her gaze from the circles underscoring her gray eyes to the sparkling beadwork at the gown's neckline. Though she'd been in for preliminary measurements, the bodice was too snug. She should've known better than to seek solace in the arms of salt-and-vinegar potato chips.

Then again, as a side effect of fertility treatments, Rachel had already gained a cumulative fifteen pounds. Why castigate herself over three more? She'd diet after the New Year like the rest of the free world. For now, she'd simply do her best to get through the next three weeks and invest in some bulge-minimizing undergarments for the wedding. Visions of Spandex body shapers danced in her head. On the big day, all eyes would be on the bride anyway.

For just a second, her memories reverted to her own walk down the aisle four and a half years ago. The sanctuary doors had opened, and despite the dozens of people present, her gaze had gone straight to David standing at the front of the church. Dark-haired and blue-eyed, he'd been impossibly handsome in his tuxedo. It was the smile, the way he'd beamed at her, though, that had made him breathtaking.

When she'd made the painful decision after Thanksgiving to separate from her husband, it had been in part because she couldn't remember the last time she'd seen that smile. The two of them had become so much less than they once were, than they should have been.

Marshaling her expression into a smile, Rachel smoothed a few wayward strands of her long black hair and drew aside the curtain. "Ta-da."

Lilah Baum clapped her hands to her cheeks, like a little girl delighted with what Santa had left. For a moment, the auburn-haired woman resembled the fourth-graders she taught. "Oh, *Rachel.* You look just beautiful! Everything is going to be so…so…" She fanned her fingers in front of her face, trying to stem tears as she sobbed something apologetic.

Behind Lilah, twenty-three-year-old Arianne Waide rolled her eyes with wry affection, looking a lot like her oldest brother. "She's a little emotional lately."

The maid of honor, petite and blond Arianne wore a dress that was completely different from Rachel's but cut from the same green satin. Clover, the seamstress had called the color. Arianne and Lilah were longtime friends who would be sisters-in-law by the end of the month. For the past four and a half years, Arianne had been Rachel's sister-in-law, too. Rachel was closer to the young woman than she was to her actual sister back in South Carolina. Throughout Lilah and Tanner's engagement, Arianne had joked that at long last, women would outnumber the men in the Waide family.

Her eyes stinging again, Rachel ducked her head. "Nothing wrong with being sentimental, especially right before your wedding."

"Yeah, but it's not *your* wedding." Arianne stepped closer while Lilah dug a tissue out of her purse. She lowered her voice, her pixie features unusually somber. "You okay?"

God, no. Ending a marriage had to be painful at any time or place, but here in the close-knit community of Mistletoe, Georgia, surrounded by people who loved her and David and didn't know they lived in opposite sides of their house, made it impossible for her to start the grieving process and move forward. Mercifully, in a few days she'd get some respite. She'd leaped at the chance to house-sit while a neighbor with multiple dogs took a fourteen-day luxury cruise. It provided Rachel a socially plausible excuse for not sleeping under the same roof as her husband, not that she'd been sleeping much.

On the plus side, she was providing tons of job security for people who manufactured under-eye concealer.

"I bet I can guess what's wrong," Ari said softly.

"Really?" Rachel's heart skipped a beat. It was bad enough she and David shouldered this secret, an ironic final intimacy; she didn't want to burden Arianne with it.

"Maybe it'll happen *next* month." Arianne squeezed her hand. "I just know you guys will make wonderful parents."

Rachel choked back a semihysterical laugh. *She thinks I started my period.* It was true that, for months, she'd thought that glimpsing those first telltale signs of blood was the most upsetting thing that could happen to her. She'd recently revised her opinion.

"Someone's gonna have to help me with this blankety-blank zipper," came a cantankerous voice from the third dressing room. "I ain't as limber as I used to be."

Lilah had blotted her eyes and was now grinning. "On my way, Vonda!"

If Lilah's bridal party wasn't the most eclectic ever seen in Mistletoe, Georgia, it had to be in the running. Top five, easily. She had thirty-year-old Rachel, a woman who would be trying to look anywhere but at her own husband during the wedding; a maid of honor who constantly joked that after growing up with two older brothers, you couldn't pay her to live with a man willingly again; second-grade teacher Quinn Keller, who had the face of an angel and an unexpectedly devilish sense of humor; and seventy-four-year-old Vonda Simms Kerrigan, a town fixture who'd had a hand in Lilah and Tanner's courtship last winter. The woman was a spitfire who won nearly every card game she played and dated younger men, or as she put it, "hotties in their sixties."

"Sorry I'm late!" Quinn said breathlessly as a saleswoman escorted her past the mirrored dais toward the fitting rooms. "Our meeting ran over." She was on a committee bringing Christmas to local families in need.

Rachel nodded toward the space she'd just vacated. "You can use that one."

No doubt Quinn would look sensational in her dress. Rather than try to find a gown that would suit four differing body types and ages, Lilah had asked the seamstress to create three individual dresses and, for Vonda, a suit. Quinn was the only one with the figure and attitude to pull off a strapless gown in December.

As they waited for the other women to emerge, Arianne turned to Rachel. "You know what might cheer you up? Shopping! Want to hit some stores after this?"

"Um…" In the past, she would have jumped at the suggestion, but time alone with Ari might provide too much temptation to confide in someone.

"Well, think about it," Arianne said as she turned her attention toward a shelved display of shoes. She picked up a sling back. "Unless you and David have plans?"

"Nothing specific." Just awkward silence and retreating to separate corners.

If she curled up in the den with a book, he turned on the television in the front living room. If she watched TV, he went for a run. She wasn't sure if he was avoiding her because he was angry or simply trying to defuse the tension by giving her space. She wasn't even sure how she felt about it. When he was in the room with her, it was like she couldn't breathe and just wanted either of them to be *anywhere* else. Yet whenever he left, her chest hitched with the urge to call him back: *Don't go, hold me, make it better.*

But that was part of the problem, wasn't it?

She'd met him at a time in her life when she was overstressed and questioning what she wanted in life, taking a vacation from her South Carolinian life as an advertising executive in Columbia. David was a natural-born leader, evidenced by civic committees he'd headed and his volunteer duties coaching touch football in early fall and soccer in the spring. They'd barely been on two dates before he was encouraging her to let him shoulder her burdens. He'd advised her as confidently as he did five-year-olds who were confused about which goal to kick toward. It had felt like a blessing at the time.

Unfortunately, in "simplifying" her life and inviting David to gloss over her problems, Rachel had lost herself somewhere along the way. In the past year, she'd begun to question whether her husband loved her—romantically, not just dutifully—but could she really blame him for not seeing her? She wasn't even sure who she was. Resolution number one for the New Year: find out.

Chapter Two

David was stepping out of the shower that evening when he heard the tentative "Hello?" from the outer room. Reflexively, he clutched his towel around him, as if the woman on the other side of the door hadn't seen his nude body a thousand times. As if she might accidentally burst in while he was undressed and make the strain between them even worse.

The thought was truly asinine on all levels. When was the last time Rachel had "burst in" anywhere? Since the miscarriage last spring, it seemed as if even rising from her chair took effort. And how on earth would it be possible for the awkwardness between them to become *worse?*

"In here," he called back.

"Okay. Just checking." Her words were followed by retreating footsteps.

He dried off and dressed, keeping his movements slow and deliberate so that he didn't impulsively run after her. The caveman deep inside him seemed to think that tossing his wife onto the bed and making thorough love to her would somehow resurrect what they'd once shared.

Stupid caveman.

The once sexy part of their marriage had long become regulated by ovulation predictor kits, and each fruitless encounter was more perfunctory and less satisfying than the last.

So what now, genius? In school he'd excelled at problem-solving. As it turned out, participating in teen extracurricular activities for gifted students and graduating college with honors didn't educate a man on understanding women. He'd tried so damn hard to be the perfect husband, and she'd just…walked away. Had she really become so numb that she had no feelings left for him?

As he walked down the hall, he heard her in the kitchen, the sound of the refrigerator door opening and closing. Her back was to him as he rounded the corner into the room. She poured herself some tea, presumably to wash down a couple of the aspirin in the big white bottle she held. Her shoulders were slumped in a defeated posture that tugged at his heart.

He used to hug her whenever she'd had a bad day, cajole her into a better mood. *Cheer up,* he'd say, *you still have me.* If he tried to embrace her now, would she stiffen and pull away?

"How was the dress fitting?" he heard himself ask. Inane small talk as if he were killing time on an elevator with a casual acquaintance.

His wife turned in his direction but didn't quite meet his eyes, addressing one of the light-stained wood cabinets just past his left shoulder. "Lilah will make a beautiful bride."

"Tanner's a lucky man."

She nodded, her fingers trembling a little as she tried to get the lid off the aspirin.

"Let me." He walked toward her, palm extended.

She recoiled. "I can do it."

"Dammit, Rachel—" Her vulnerable expression quelled the reactionary anger that had been rising in him.

She looked somehow both harder and more fragile than the woman he'd once known. Her eyes were shadowed, and there was a chafed spot on her bottom lip. She had a bad habit of chewing on her lip when she was upset. He glanced up in sudden realization that he was staring at her mouth and she'd caught him doing it.

Defensiveness made his tone gruff. "You look like hell."

Her normally warm gray eyes were the color of cold steel. "Thank you so much."

"I didn't…" He ran a hand through his hair. "I just worry about you."

"That's not your responsibility anymore," she said with an attempt at a smile, as if she was trying to point out a positive.

His pride—*his heart*—stung. "I guess we can't all just turn off our emotions and walk away from vows so easily."

For a second, he thought she might throw the aspirin bottle at him. Instead, she turned toward the counter, dismissing him with her body language.

He clenched his fists at his sides. He'd known this woman for years. Laughed with her, loved her, said things to her he couldn't imagine sharing with another person. Yet the prospect of beating himself upside the head with one of the pots hanging over the kitchen island seemed less painful than a three-minute conversation with her. How had they come to this?

"I'm sorry," he said. He rarely lost his temper, and he needed his composure now more than ever. "That was uncalled for."

"You're entitled to your anger." With an audible pop, the lid finally came off the bottle. "It'll be easier when I'm at Winnie's. I'm supposed to go over tonight to spend time with the animals and look over all the instructions with her."

"Yeah, she phoned to say she was in for the evening and any time was good with her. And your sister called. That's what I came in here to tell you." Probably he should have led with that rather than *You look like hell*. "She said it was important, but not bad news."

Considering the massive heart attack that had threatened Mr. Nietermyer's life the year David met Rachel, and the two lesser cardiac episodes that had followed, urgent messages from home tended to make her nervous.

"Thanks." She washed down two pills with a gulp, placed her cup on the counter, then turned, clearly ready to take her leave of him.

He didn't move aside. "Did you grab a bite with the ladies?"

"No, Lilah had dinner plans, and everyone else went shopping. I didn't feel up to it."

"I'll fix you something. You should—"

"David." She smiled tiredly. "Thank you, but I'm a big girl. I'm capable of opening my own aspirin and cooking my own meals."

Of course she was. He was just so desperate to *do*

something. For most of his life, he'd enjoyed a sense of purpose. His mom had raised him with the notion that he could do anything he set his mind to, and for nearly thirty years, that had held true. Then there'd come the infertility problems, which had made him crazy because there was nothing he could do to help Rach, and then her announcement that she was leaving. He'd been so dumbfounded, so struck by the unfamiliar sensation of being out of control, that he'd just let her go.

Part of him—if he were being brutally honest— might even have been relieved by the time apart, but only as a stopgap measure, not as a permanent life change.

"When you call your sister back, you aren't going to tell her about us, are you?" It sounded autocratic even in his own ears, a demand. He couldn't bear anyone knowing that his marriage had failed. Every person who found out would be one more severed tie cutting him adrift.

Rachel glared, exasperated. "I don't know. I agreed with you that this is a special time for Lilah and Tanner, the whole Waide family, and I didn't want to ruin it. But don't you think I deserve a friendly ear? Someone to talk to?"

Why hadn't she tried harder to talk to *him?* He'd always listened, always offered suggestions and attempted to soothe the problems away. "Rachel. You know that if it were in my power to—"

"I know." She surprised him by reaching out, brushing her hand over the arm of his long-sleeved T-shirt. Then she passed by, not looking back as she added, "But it's not."

BECAUSE a chilly December rain had started to fall, Rachel drove to Winnie's on the other side of the sub-division rather than walk. When the windshield wipers did nothing to clear her view, she realized the spots blurring her vision were tears. This was ridiculous. Sep-arating was *her* decision, yet she'd cried every day since she'd told David that they didn't belong together.

Despite what logic and intellect told her, on some level she felt she'd failed by not getting pregnant. Why couldn't her body accomplish what some teenagers achieved unintentionally? When she'd suffered a first-trimester miscarriage last spring, it had devastated her, yet she'd tried to see it as a sign that at least she could conceive. But month after month, hope waned. As did her and David's tenderness with each other. She could admit that there had been some hormone-triggered mood swings on her part and that she'd been difficult to live with. He'd been patient at first, but no sooner had she lost a child than he began touting adoption as the reasonable solution. His seemingly "just get over it" attitude trivialized everything she'd experienced and made her feel alone even when he was holding her... which was less and less.

David liked to tell people what course of action they should take, whether it was customers at his family's store, his newly returned brother or councilmen at town meetings. Almost everyone valued his input; Rachel herself had sought his opinion in the early days of marriage. It had taken her until this year to realize how aloof he could be when people didn't follow his advice.

She hadn't been able to shake the feeling that he didn't view her as an equal partner.

Tonight was one example of how an endearing habit could turn grating. She'd once found it charming that he would remind her to eat or do little things to take care of her, but lately his suggestions had begun to sound slightly condescending.

Her heart rate kicked up suddenly, her pulse pounding in her ears so loudly that she couldn't hear her own thoughts—not an altogether bad thing considering their dark tone. Her vision swam. *What the hell?* Fingers clenched on the steering wheel, she hurriedly parked at the curb. Then she waited, taking deep breaths.

Was she being melodramatic, or had she just almost fainted? She'd never passed out in her life. Though her headache remained in full force, her pulse slowed enough that she could walk to Winnie's front door and ring the bell without worrying that she looked like a deranged escapee from the nearest hospital.

Winnie Brisbane, receptionist for the town veterinarian, was one of the softest-hearted people in the county. Her two lab mixes had been with her for years; a three-legged cat named Arpeggio and a lop-eared rabbit were more recent additions. Winnie had been negotiating with local pet-sitter Brenna Pierce to care for the menagerie when she'd found an abandoned puppy in a November storm. Though she'd placed a poster in the vet's office, most people were too preoccupied with approaching holiday chaos to take on a gangly puppy with a nervous bladder and no obedience training. By Thanksgiving, Winnie had named the mutt Hildie.

Short of Winnie canceling the cruise she and her cousins had been planning for over a year, having someone house-sit seemed the only sensible solution. Brenna's client schedule was too full for the constant care a puppy required, not to mention how much the extra professional visits would stretch Winnie's modest budget. She'd laughingly told Rachel that she'd blown this year's mad money on cruise wear and was making up for it with peanut-butter-sandwich lunches and macaroni-and-cheese dinners.

"The dogs are officially eating better than I am," she'd admitted when Rachel offered to puppy-sit.

As Winnie ushered her into the house, Rachel had a twinge of guilt over the woman's outpouring of gratitude. Though there was no good way to explain it to sweet-natured, freckle-faced Winnie, who blushed when David so much as smiled, Rachel had taken the house-sitting gig for selfish reasons. Tonight it had hit home how impossible it was for her to be under the same roof with her husband and not just because their exchanges deteriorated into sniping or unproductive regrets.

When he'd walked into the kitchen earlier, she'd been overwhelmed, out of the blue, by the sandalwood scent of his shampoo. Her sense of smell seemed abnormally strong, maybe because of the headache. She'd read about people with migraines having heightened sensitivities. Whatever the cause, she'd had a nearly visceral memory of him washing her hair once, the feel of his hands across her scalp, the rich lather of the shampoo, his soapy skin sliding against hers as they leaned together for a kiss, the water sluicing over both their bodies.

"Rachel? Are you okay?"

Good heavens, she'd completely forgotten about Winnie sitting across the table, summarizing pet routines that were written in a spiral notebook.

"Sorry." Rachel swallowed. "I got a little…overheated for a moment. Can I trouble you for a glass of water?"

Winnie made a sympathetic noise. "Those medications, I expect."

One of the positives of living in a small town was that people *cared*—when they asked how you were doing, they wanted an honest answer, not a rote "fine, thanks." Susan Waide, strongly in favor of becoming a grandmother, had asked for prayer support among her friends at church on David and Rachel's behalf. The OB's office staff knew Rachel by name and were all pulling for her. Sometimes, having everyone within shouting distance knowing the details of her life and cheering her on was nice.

This was not one of those times.

So she kept it to herself that she wasn't even taking the drugs anymore; she'd emptied her last prescription just prior to Halloween. The doctors had warned then that potential long-term dangers of the hormones were starting to outweigh the possibility of conception. They'd broached the subject of in vitro procedures, but she'd decided against it pretty early in the discussion process. It was expensive, offered no guarantees, and frankly, her relationship with David had cooled so much by then that she wondered if it would be fair to bring a baby into their home.

Home. Glad Winnie stood at the sink with her back

turned, Rachel surreptitiously wiped away tears. When David had surprised her late in their engagement with the key to the brick house two streets over, she'd thought it was her dream home. Now it stood as a museum of their disappointments and mistakes.

The sooner I get out of that house, the better. She found herself reciting the mantra several times a day. She just wished she could convince herself it was true.

WHEN Rachel returned from Winnie's, David was hunched over his laptop in the front living room, no doubt working on files for the store. The Waides had owned a supply store in Mistletoe for generations, but it had really grown under David and Zachariah's partnership. In the spring, Zachariah Waide had gone into partial retirement, handing over the bulk of daily management to his oldest child. David had thrown himself into the job with gusto, seeming happier when he was at the store than he did when he was with her.

Careful not to disturb his work now, Rachel tiptoed past, stealing one undisciplined peek at his chiseled profile, bathed in blue from the monitor's glow in the darkened room. How many pictures had she taken of that face, trying to capture perfectly on film the strength and character there? It was so unfair. While she'd been mourning the loss of her chic but no longer necessary professional wardrobe and grappling with some unattractive side effects of the medicine, David merely got sexier with each passing day. He'd doubled his jogging regimen, and now that Tanner was back, David was shooting hoops regularly in addition to the community softball he'd always played. He was in the best shape of his adult life, which made her feel even worse that her own body had turned against her.

She didn't realize she was holding her breath until she got to the guest room at the end of the house and finally exhaled. It was such a pretty room really, the muted pastels in the drapes and matching queen-size comforter off-setting the dark wood of the sleigh bed. A person should feel cheerful here. A person should not obsess over how this room would have made a lovely nursery.

After the miscarriage, Rachel had fallen into the habit of coming here when she couldn't sleep, just to sit and think, then she'd awake on the bed in the morning. David never said a word about it, so when difficulties between them had reached their zenith, it had been almost a natural transition to adopt this room as her own. She hadn't actually started moving clothes into the closet and her alarm clock onto the nightstand until after Thanksgiving, when she'd told him she couldn't do this anymore.

She would miss a lot of things when it came time to leave Mistletoe—friends, the Waides, the chicken-fried steak down at Dixieland Diner—but she would not miss this room. Grabbing the cordless phone, she sat on the mattress. She should return Kate's call before it got too late.

Her younger sister, who lived with her husband and eleven-month-old daughter just a few miles from Rachel's parents, picked up on the first ring. "Hello?"

"Hey, it's Rachel. David said you called?"

"Oh, hi!" Kate's greeting was so effusive that it

bordered on a squeal. Odd. The last few times they'd spoken, her sister had been subtly petulant that Rachel wasn't coming to South Carolina for Christmas. After all, it would be little Alyssa's first, never mind that Rachel had committed to being in a wedding and was planning to visit home for New Year's. Rachel had even contemplated getting out of Mistletoe for Thanksgiving, but Kate had gone to her in-laws' place in Virginia so that they could coo over the grand-baby.

"You sound like you're in a good mood," Rachel observed.

"The *best!* I'm so glad you called back. I'm having lunch with Mom tomorrow, so I'll talk to her then, but she heard first the last time. I thought it should be your turn."

Rachel couldn't help smiling, Kate's fast-paced prattle reminding her of when they were younger and her sister would burst through the kitchen door with sixty-miles-an-hour news of her day. "My turn for what?"

"Okay, you are officially the very first person in the family to hear this." Kate giggled. "Well, except for Mike, obviously. He bought the test for me."

"Test?" Rachel's stomach dropped. Realization hit. *I am the worst sister in the world.* She didn't want to hear this news; she wanted to slam down the phone and curl into the fetal position. Pun not intended.

"We're expecting again! Alyssa is going to be a big sister. It's a little sooner than we anticipated—I mean, we just started trying and you never know how long it will…" Kate trailed off in abashed silence.

"Congratulations," Rachel said. "That's wonderful."

"I am so sorry." Kate sounded horrified. "That was

a really insensitive way to put that. I was just so excited—"

"As you should be! And you were right, a woman never does know how long it will take." *Or if it will happen, ever.* "Don't worry. I'd be a lousy person if I weren't thrilled for you."

"You're sure?"

Hell. Once again, tears threatened to well in Rachel's eyes—what was that, the sixth time today?—but she was determined not to let Fertile Myrtle know. She coughed, trying to keep her voice even. "Absolutely! I owe you a huge congratulatory hug when I see you in January."

"Yeah, you'll want to do it then before I get too big to wrap your arms around," Kate joked.

They talked for a few more minutes, but it was clear that neither one of them was entirely comfortable.

"Oh, dear," Kate said, interrupting as Rachel answered a question about Lilah's wedding plans. "That's Alyssa crying. I'd better go. See you in a few weeks!"

"Right. See you then." Rachel disconnected, flopped back on the mattress and glared at the ceiling.

Well, at least now when she announced to her parents—who were already baffled as to why she was "wasting" her college degree in a "dinky" North Georgia town—that her marriage had crashed and burned, the Nietermyers would have Kate's pregnancy as a happy distraction.

Yeah, that made Rachel feel *much* better.

Chapter Three

Mental note. Rachel squeezed herself behind a kitchen chair for safety. *Never, never ask a bunch of animals "Who wants to go for a walk?"*

Unless, of course, she *wanted* to be trampled to death. The two labs were scrambling to reach her, and Hildie was probably waking up the neighborhood, running circles on the tile and barking her head off. Although the dogs enjoyed playing in their own fenced backyard, Winnie had mentioned that walks were a special treat. Bristol and Rembrandt shared a double-dog leash, and in theory, Rachel should be able to walk Hildie with her own leash held in the other hand.

Faced with the challenge of harnessing all this uncoordinated enthusiasm, however, Rachel was suddenly dubious. If she had any common sense, she'd probably be snuggled under the covers; she wasn't due for work at the print shop for another two and a half hours.

But she hadn't been asleep anyway. She'd been up three times during the night, probably because the unfamiliar noises of pets in the house kept waking her. Shortly before 6:00 a.m., it had become clear that no matter how exhausted she was, she was awake for the duration.

Awake and cowering behind furniture.

She cleared her throat, hoping to project authority. "Sit. I mean it, you guys. Sit!"

The labs' collective butts hit the floor, their tails sweeping in noisy arcs. Hildie continued to run in demented circles, woofing happily. *Two out of three is close enough.* Rachel edged from behind the chair, maintaining stern eye contact while she picked up the leashes. She shrugged into a flannel-lined, double-breasted coat. It was bulky, especially over her blue sweat suit, but it was indisputably soft, as if she were walking around in a much-needed hug.

Though she'd never been a morning person, there was something surprisingly invigorating about stepping outside into the chilly air, watching the sun rise in golden-orange streaks that gilded the clouds. *That would make a pretty picture.* Even if she hadn't busted her camera last month, she didn't exactly have a free hand right now. And the dogs definitely lacked the patience for her to stop and take in picturesque scenes— they were already straining against their leashes.

They set off at a brisk pace, Rachel's breath puffing out in foggy bursts. If she was lucky, she might even lose a pound or two before the wedding and her trip home. Should she return to South Carolina at her current weight, her mom—a slim woman with a closet full of Power Suits—would cluck her tongue disapprovingly. Mrs. Nietermyer had mastered the many fine nuances of Clucking 101. Mr. Nietermyer habitually called his wife *honey,* but Rachel swore that, once or twice, what he'd really said was *henny.*

Lost in her thoughts and the steady rhythm of the dogs' toes clicking on the pavement, she was startled when Hildie shot after a trio of sparrows.

"Whoa!" Rachel gripped the leash tightly. "Sit. *Sit.*"

No one listened. Instead, Hildie's sudden dash whipped the other two dogs into a fervor. They quickly tangled their lines, threatening to ensnare Rachel. She managed to sidestep Bristol, but tripped over Rembrandt. Falling toward the sidewalk, Rachel reflexively braced herself with one hand. Which was, she acknowledged as pain radiated up her arm, stupid. She was lucky she hadn't broken her wrist. Of more immediate concern, however, was that, in thrusting her hand out, she'd let go of Hildie's leash. The little terror went flopping toward the spot where the birds had been.

Dammit. Cold seeped through the layers of cotton covering her butt.

Rachel got to her feet and approached the puppy slowly, not wanting to chase her into the intersection. Though it was still early, some people would be leaving for work soon and the dog wouldn't be easily visible in the early-morning light. Scanning the area for any threats or surprises, Rachel sidled toward the mutt. When movement caught her eye, she turned and saw someone cresting the hill on the parallel sidewalk. A jogger, whose gait and clothes she recognized even at a distance.

She'd always thought that particular blue T-shirt brought out the color in her husband's eyes. Her heart thumped against her ribs. She turned to Hildie. "If you will come to me *right now,* I swear you can have as many puppy treats as you want when we get home."

Hildie yipped once, scooting farther away and wagging her tail in appreciation of the new game.

"Dog, I am not playing with you. Get over here." Now the footsteps across the street were audible. *Slap, slap. Slap, slap.* Rachel squeezed her eyes shut. Maybe she wasn't actually outside at dawn with three dogs who'd alternately tried to escape and hog-tie her. Maybe she was simply having a nightmare. Her dreams, when she slept long enough to have them, *had* been bizarrely vivid of late.

"Rach?" Opposite her, David slowed to a stop. The inquisitive note in his voice probably stemmed from wondering why the heck she was out stalking an ill-behaved puppy instead of comfortably drinking coffee in Winnie's kitchen while the dogs cavorted in their own backyard. Rachel was wondering the same thing herself.

"I didn't expect to see you here," she said. She'd been so relieved to be out of the oppressive atmosphere in their house that she hadn't considered she would be walking dogs in the same neighborhood where he routinely ran. Somewhat unnecessarily, she added, "Hildie got away from me."

Hearing her name, the adolescent mongrel yipped again, sounding proud of herself. Rachel entertained a couple of fantasies that would probably not be appreciated by animal activists. David rocked back on his heels, his fledgling smile achingly familiar yet a little surprising, too. There was real amusement there and less of the strain she'd become accustomed to seeing.

"Need a little help?" he called.

"Thanks, but I've got it. You probably just got your pulse rate in the right zone or whatever. Don't let us derail you." Wrapping the remaining leash tightly around her hand, she crouched down and whistled at Hildie. "Here, girl! C'mere, baby."

Hildie took about two steps in Rachel's direction, then turned and dashed across another yard, into the Stephensons' driveway.

There was a muffled laugh from David's direction, and Rachel snapped her head toward him, heat blooming in her cheeks.

As David crossed the street, her pride warred with practicality. The charm of the early-morning walk had faded, and Rachel was looking forward to getting out of the cold and spending a few dog-free moments in a hot shower. He stepped up on the curb, extending a hand so carefully that she might have laughed if she weren't so miserable. Something about David's manner mirrored the way she was advancing on the skittish dog.

Up close, Rachel couldn't help noticing the slight crinkle of laugh lines at the corners of his eyes. He had a great face. Masculine and friendly and reassuring and sexy all at the same time. Sometimes she just—

"Here, let me at least hold the other two while you round up the little one."

She nodded, untangling the leash from her hand and passing it to him. David's fingers closed over hers. *Zing.* In the early rays of the morning, with two labs watching her as if she was a moron and an un-disciplined puppy leading her on a merry chase,

Rachel Waide experienced the most surprising jolt.
David's fingers were warm but the tiniest bit rough—
no girly moisturizing lotion for him, thank you very
much—and the scent of him was musky and male.
Her pheromones reacted with an interest they hadn't
shown in months, causing an actual twinge between
her thighs.

Her jaw dropped.

"You all right?" David narrowed his eyes, scruti-
nizing her.

Oh, please, please, don't let him be able tell. Did he
know her well enough to guess that she was unbe-
lievably, unmistakably aroused? She was mortified. Was
she one of those emotionally stunted people who only
wanted someone they couldn't have? Why was she
having this inconvenient reaction now?

Maybe it was a Pavlovian response. After all, he was
the only man she'd been with in years, and her body hadn't
yet adjusted to the idea of never touching him again. Never
kissing him, never waking in his arms, never—

Hildie barked, mercifully interrupting the mental
tangent. Circling the dog, Rachel spoke in a nonstop,
cajoling murmur, forcing herself to stand patiently as
Hildie got closer. Inch by irritating inch. Rachel waited
until she knew with absolute certainty that victory was
in her reach before she pounced, catching the wiggling
puppy in her hands. Hildie's brown eyes were wide as
she licked Rachel's cheek.

"Don't bother with the cute," Rachel warned. "You
are in big trouble, young lady."

David met her halfway, giving her the other leashes

along with a curious once-over. "So, you're settled in okay at Winnie's?"

Rachel nodded. "Yeah, I'm good."

"Really?"

No, not really. But she had to learn how to stand on her own two feet again. She moved her shoulders in a noncommittal shrug.

He bent at the waist, doing a few stretches in preparation for resuming his run. "Well, maybe we'll meet like this again."

She laughed ruefully. "I hope not! Somehow I don't think morning walks are going to become a habit."

"Guess not." His smiled had faded. "See you at my parents' on Friday?"

The whole family was gathering to trim the Christmas tree. She could make an excuse to get out of it, except she'd skipped it last year. As she recalled, that had been the day she'd learned she wasn't pregnant— again—and the thought of pretending to be in a festive, holiday mood… Not that this would be her most festive year, but it would be her last Christmas as a Waide. Was it selfish to want these final precious memories, to store them away in a mental scrapbook?

Maybe one day she could reexamine those memories and remember just the warmth and good times, without the paralyzing grief.

"I'll be there," she said. They'd also see each other on Saturday, but there'd be a bigger crowd at the party for Lilah and Tanner so maybe it wouldn't be too awkward. *Who are you kidding?* She'd be attending a couples' shower with her estranged husband.

David nodded. "See you this weekend, then."

As he started off again, she added, "Thanks for your help. I'm grateful our paths crossed."

He smiled over his shoulder, but didn't answer. She stared after his back, wondering how he felt.

Down the road, would he be glad that their paths had crossed five years ago, that he'd overcome her laughing protestations that she was only in town for a short while and had no plans to get involved with someone here? Or would he end up wishing he'd simply stayed on his side of the street and let the woman from South Carolina pass by without disrupting his life?

DAVID GRIMACED as he reached for the canister of coffee high in the supply cabinet. His sore muscles protested. Maybe he didn't need caffeine that badly after all. Maybe what he needed was to stop pushing himself as if he were an indestructible kid half his age. After his encounter with Rachel, he'd sprinted a double circuit through the subdivision, trying to outrun the effect of seeing her.

She'd looked disarming and maddeningly adorable, all bundled up. Her eyes had been bright, almost silvery, and spots of color had livened a face that had been far too pale for far too long. This morning she'd reminded him of the woman he'd married, not the much quieter, pinched version she'd become. Seeing the improvement one night had made, he was forced to conclude that she'd been right—she *was* better off without him. A groan of enraged despair rumbled in his throat.

"David?" His mother's voice, lilting in question, startled him. He'd thought he was alone in the employees-only hallway behind the store.

"Mom." His arms dropped quickly to his sides, as if she'd caught him reaching for forbidden cookies. "I didn't know you were in this morning."

"Brought over some more ornaments for Ari to display. You do a great job running the store, just like your father always has, but neither of you excel when it comes to decorating for the customers."

Decorating. He thought about his house, which was completely devoid of holiday cheer. Their first year of marriage, Rachel had barely waited for Thanksgiving before she started asking if it was too soon to put up Christmas lights. She'd seemed so happy then, as he'd promised her she'd be if she moved here to Mistletoe, enthusiastic to build their life together.

Susan brought him back to the present. "Why were you growling in the hallway?"

"I, uh, can't reach the coffee."

She skewered him with a raised eyebrow, then turned to open the janitorial closet behind her, revealing a small step stool that he'd known perfectly well was there. "God knows I love your brother and how spirited he is, but he was the one more likely to stubbornly pursue the impossible with no real plan on how to achieve it. You were the solution-finder."

Really? Because David was fresh out of solutions. Feeling foolish, he picked up the stool and retrieved the coffee. "Lack of caffeine makes me grouchy. And stupid."

Susan Waide's gaze was steady, all-knowing in that way mothers have. "Want to tell me what's really wrong?"

"Thanks, Mom, but it's nothing that can be fixed with a step stool."

"You and Rachel?"

His pulse pounded. How much of the truth had she guessed? "Is it that obvious that we've…hit a rough patch?"

"Oh, darling." She ruffled his hair, even though she practically had to stand on tiptoe to do it. "I can't imagine how difficult it was for her to lose that baby, but she's been withdrawn for months. And you've been tense, short-fused. Not at all the boy I know."

He missed the man he'd been, the one who had never questioned his wife's love and their ability to work through any problem.

"Every couple has difficulties," Susan continued. "Lord knows your father and I have. It's healthy even. Once you work through to the other side, you'll be stronger for it."

He opened his mouth, then closed it. His biggest fear was that for him and Rachel, there was no other side. *I shouldn't have let her go.* He could have convinced her to at least sleep on it or maybe see a counselor together. Would fighting for her now be the right thing to do or merely the selfish?

"Mom." He hugged his mother, his voice ragged. It was nearly impossible to spit out the question. "What if—what if I can't fix this?"

"Nonsense. You're my son. Besides—" she smiled up at him "—you're forgetting that it's Christmas. The season of miracles."

"HERE YA GO, Chloe." Rachel passed the box of business cards over the counter. "Why don't you take a peek at the first few and make sure they're to your satisfaction?"

"Oh, I'm sure that's not necessary." Chloe Malcolm glanced at the sample card stapled to the outside of the box. "You always do a great job."

Once, Rachel had helped create regional ad campaigns for a major company. Now, it was an exciting day if she got to help someone lay out business cards—except that Chloe, who ran her own small company as a Web designer, rarely needed help. She'd brought in her file on CD, all ready to be printed. There was nothing at work challenging enough to distract Rachel from her embarrassing encounter with David earlier. Of course, there was the special project she should be working on for Lilah and Tanner's rehearsal dinner, but she doubted that would improve her mood.

Rachel shook her head. "You couldn't even have left a formatting error I could resolve?"

"Pardon?" The brunette blinked at her.

"Don't mind me. Midday blahs," she told Chloe. "I'm waiting for May to come back so I can take my lunch break. To tell you the truth, the day so far has been pretty monotonous."

"Not too much action going on in Mistletoe, huh?" Chloe sounded wistful, which was surprising. Gifted with computers, the young woman was also incredibly introverted; she'd always given the impression she might panic at the first sign of "action."

They both glanced reflexively toward the door when it opened, and Rachel's co-worker May Gideon swept inside, accompanied by a winter-edged breeze. The pungent odor of a fried fish sandwich wafted from May's white paper bag, and Rachel's gut clenched. Her hand shot to her mouth.

"Whoa." Chloe was blinking again. "You look really pale."

"I, uh…I—" Terrified that she was about to humiliate herself far worse than she had that morning with the runaway puppy, Rachel bolted for the employee restroom. After splashing some cold water on her face and taking a couple of deep breaths, she managed to quell the intense nausea. It was gone almost as suddenly as it had come. Still, she waited a few minutes to make sure.

When she returned to the front of the print shop, she saw that May had completed Chloe's transaction and was now arguing with Mrs. Nugent, who wanted them to make a personalized photo calendar as a Christmas present for her mother, but refused to accept that they weren't allowed to reproduce copyrighted pictures of her kids.

"After what that studio charged me for the darn things, I should be able to wallpaper my whole house with them if I want to!"

May's patient expression didn't waver. "So long as you understand that we can't print the wallpaper for you."

This seemed like as good a time as any for Rachel to take her lunch hour. With a guilty half wave in May's direction, she crept toward the door, not wanting to get caught up in Mrs. Nugent's righteous indignation over the "highway robbery" of professional photography. Once Rachel was outside and contemplating where to go for lunch, she admitted to herself that food was the last thing she wanted.

Finally, something good about stress—it had her stomach so upset it was killing her appetite. Maybe she'd fit into that bridesmaid's dress after all.

A niggling voice in the back of her head pointed out she'd been stressed all morning, yet hadn't been in danger of tossing her cookies until that fish smell hit. It was similar to last spring, when… She stopped dead on the sidewalk. What a ridiculous thought. Still, now that she considered it, when had her last period been? Rachel bit her lip, not sure. For the first time in nearly two years, she wasn't obsessively tracking her cycle, trying hard to let go and reach a healthier emotional state.

Oh, yeah, I'm a picture of mental health. She gave a quick shake of her head. Now that she was off the medications that had regulated her cycles, it wasn't surprising that she might skip a period—or two?—as her body adjusted. In fact, her bursting into tears at the drop of a hat lately and her sensory overreaction to odors was probably just PMS. She'd start her period any day and feel silly about this.

Yep. An-n-ny day now.

Chapter Four

"Hey, Rach! Come in where it's warm." Arianne opened the door of her parents' house. She lived in a garage apartment these days—Susan kept saying she and Zachariah didn't need all the space, but they couldn't bear to put the family home up for sale even though it was just the two of them there. "It's finally starting to feel like December, isn't it? David's inside getting a fire started."

Rachel had seen his car out front; he'd probably come straight from work. A stray memory broadsided her of her husband wanting to create a romantic scene by lighting their first fire in their new home and making love in its glow on the living room sofa. But it had been a ridiculously warm winter that year, and to make the house cold enough, he'd cranked up the air-conditioning. That was David, determined to control his environment.

Then again, there was something to be said for a man who worked that hard to create a romantic moment for his wife. He'd met her while she was vacationing in Mistletoe, and knowing their time together might be temporary, he'd systematically pulled out all the stops in wooing her. He'd—

"Rachel?" Arianne prompted.

She started guiltily, as if she'd been caught committing a crime instead of daydreaming about her own spouse. "I had to let the dogs out! Winnie's dogs, I mean. Th-that's why David and I arrived separately."

"Yeah, we know." Arianne studied her, looking perplexed.

Well, subterfuge never was my strong suit. Shrugging out of her coat, Rachel scooted past her sister-in-law to greet the rest of the family, which was segregated along gender lines. She heard Tanner and Zachariah offering unsolicited advice on how to arrange the logs; the women were gathered in the kitchen. Rachel made a beeline for the latter and hung her jacket over the back of a chair. Her black jeans and red scoop-necked sweater certainly fitted in the overall color scheme.

Lilah sat at the table in a casual red dress chopping carrots, while Susan, wearing a white-and-red checkered cardigan over dark slacks, seasoned the pot of stew on the stove. The dishwasher stood ajar. Since Arianne hated to cook, Rachel bet her sister-in-law's job had been unloading dishes.

"Smells divine in here." Rachel kissed her mother-in-law's cheek.

She'd always admired Susan's aura of balance and domestic elegance. The woman seemed comfortable at home cooking for her husband, but equally capable when she was juggling volunteer work in town and at the store. Rachel's own mom had fought hard to be successful in the workplace, devoting a lot of energy to her career. Though Rachel hadn't questioned whether she was loved, Mrs. Nietermyer had never seemed completely, well, *motherly*. As a girl, Rachel had thought her mother harbored an unspoken disdain for homemakers, as if they weren't as smart or driven. But Susan Waide was sharp as a tack, and Rachel now wondered if what she'd perceived from her mom had been, in part, jealousy…envy over skills she herself couldn't seem to master.

What kind of mother would I have made? Her chest tightened at the thought, and she pushed away the painful "what if." "What can I do to help?"

"We're pretty well set in here," Susan said. "Could you go remind Zachariah that he and Tanner were supposed to put the extra leaf in the dining room table?"

"Arianne and I can probably take care of that."

"I appreciate the offer," Susan said as Ari resumed putting away pots and pans. "But if the boys plan to eat with us, they have to do their part. It won't hurt them to work for it, dear."

Lilah laughed. "That sounds like something Aunt Shelby would say."

Though Rachel always considered Lilah a Mistletoe native, the woman hadn't been born here like David and his siblings; she'd moved in with her aunt and uncle years ago after her parents had died in a crash. Lilah's uncle Ray would walk her down the aisle.

"That's because Shelby Tierney is very wise," Susan said approvingly. "You'll have no shortage of marital advice, if you want it. I'm always here." She swung her shrewd gaze back toward Rachel in clear invitation.

Rachel swallowed. She'd considered discussing the deteriorating state of her marriage with Susan, but it had seemed somehow disloyal to run to David's family with their problems. Weren't the Waides duty-bound to take his side? Well, maybe not Arianne. She regularly labeled her older brothers as pains in the butt.

I'll miss them all so much. She turned away. "I'll go see about having the guys set up the table."

Before Rachel reached the living room, she heard masculine laughter. From the snatches she gathered, David and his brother were teasing their father about a fire he'd once tried to start on a camping trip.

"To this day," Tanner was saying as she entered the room, "Mom still— Oh, hey, Rach." He crossed the room to hug her, so like his brother in build and coloring that her return embrace was awkward. It had been such a long time since David had held her just to be close. She used to laugh at the way he'd hug her from behind at silly times—while she was trying to put away groceries or brush her teeth. She missed those embraces, but as their married life had grown more tense, their physical relationship had withered.

Now, David watched her wordlessly from the hearth. Their gazes met, held, as the flames behind him crackled. Her stomach somersaulted, not with nausea this time but jitters. A confusing combination of dread and excitement reminiscent of a teenage crush. Zachariah Waide moved in for his hello, interrupting the visual contact.

Rachel regained her composure enough to smile up at him. "Your wife sent me to remind you about the table."

He grunted in acknowledgment. "Knew I forgot to do something. Come on, Tanner. You can help me while Rachel and David start opening boxes."

The tree stood in the corner. Someone had brought down four large containers, two cardboard and two clear plastic, of Christmas paraphernalia from the attic. After dinner, they would all help decorate. She thought of the Our New Home ornament she'd put in David's stocking their first year of marriage. It had fallen off the tree once, knocking off the chimney and cracking the roof on the little house, but he'd glued it back on, insisting the ornament was as good as new.

"Hey." He spoke first, not looking nearly as nervous as she felt.

After a moment, she realized she was studying him a bit too intently. He hitched an eyebrow questioningly.

"So." *Boxes,* Rachel told herself. Much safer to divert her attention to the boxes. "Where should we start?"

He glanced down, considering. "The lights. Might as well check to make sure they're all working before we go to the trouble of putting them on the tree."

Rachel read Susan's neat handwriting and meticulous labels. Assuming everything had been put away correctly, the lights should be in the cardboard box closest to her. She bent at the waist and unfolded the flaps.

Rachel straightened, saying over her shoulder, "Here they— What are you doing?" she demanded as David hurriedly raised his gaze.

"Hmm?" he asked, not meeting her eyes.

Rachel frowned, the tingles shivering through her making her self-conscious. Was she crazy or had he actually been ogling her butt? "Were you…"

"Just standing here. Waiting for you to hand me one end of the lights so we can plug them in." But she wasn't the only one who was bad at subterfuge. Even with his head ducked, she recognized the glint in his eyes— she'd been his lover for five years.

She couldn't help grinning at how unconvincing he was. "You lie."

"Oh, really?" He did look up then, his answering smile a challenge. "What exactly are you accusing me of?"

They both knew the answer to that, but she wasn't quite gutsy enough to vocalize it. She'd felt David pulling away physically, had thought for a while that he didn't find her attractive anymore. So, on the one hand, it was validating to catch him staring, made her feel feminine in a way she hadn't for a long time. *On the other hand,* they'd split up, even if they were the only ones here who knew that. Why confuse the issue with flirtatious conversation?

"Never mind," she backpedaled. "I was mistaken."

He moved toward her, reaching for the lights. "No, you weren't."

Please don't. She didn't want to be seduced by the mischievous note in his voice, reminded of everything good they'd shared—sure, the journey had had some high points, but that didn't change her unhappiness with where they'd arrived. And if he hadn't been just as miserable, David Waide would have fought for her.

When she'd finally dredged up the nerve to confess she didn't think their marriage was working, that it had long since become a marriage based on technicalities rather than intimacy, she'd braced herself for argument. He'd always been a man who refused to brook defeat. He'd once planted a tree that didn't successfully take root in the soil, but he'd come back with some kind of specialized fertilizer and continued watering it for weeks, not ready to acknowledge that it was dead. Rachel had anticipated that he'd tell her she was being melodramatic—whenever she'd tried during the past year to broach the difficult conversation of their not being happy, he'd turned into Mr. Optimism, automatically downplaying her fears and telling her he loved her. That they could do anything together (except possibly have a child). She wanted to appreciate his positive thinking, but it became more difficult over time in the wake of her growing frustration that he was not hearing her. After Thanksgiving, she'd been determined to make him finally listen, but she hadn't expected him to capitulate so readily. She'd anticipated his saying that things would look better in the morning, his once again proposing immediate solutions before she'd had a chance to fully articulate what she saw as the problems.

Instead, he'd practically shrugged in agreement. He'd expended more effort on the damn tree.

"Why now?" she muttered under her breath.

David paused. "What do you mean?"

She rolled her shoulders, trying to alleviate some of the growing tension.

Not even the small motion got by him. "You need one of my famous back rubs."

"I don't think so." If the mere brush of his fingers this morning had caused a zing, what would happen with her muscles warm under his touch? Annoyed by how tempting the offer sounded, she glared. "Don't flirt with me. Not now, not after months of…"

"What, not touching you?" He was even closer now,

his voice lowered to give them privacy. "You pushed me away, Rach. You made it clear you didn't want me looking at your body. Unless it was for procreation."

She flinched. During the hormone treatments, she'd tried to explain to him how the side effects sometimes made her feel like a stranger in her own skin. But David, for all that he paid lip service to "being there" for her, could grow impatient with discussions that didn't have easy answers. If she tried to tell him that she didn't feel like herself, didn't feel sexy, he'd roll his eyes and tell her that she was being neurotic, that she looked just fine to him. Somehow, being called neurotic wasn't a big turn-on for her.

"If I seemed uninterested," he continued, "I was just trying to respect your wishes. I wanted to take care of you."

"I know, David. But that's not what I wanted." They were supposed to take care of *each other,* except that he'd never seemed to need her.

"You don't consider that part of a husband's job?" He was looking distinctly irritated now. "Taking care of his wife?"

"It's a nice sentiment, but you got more and more…" Paternal? That would not sit well with him and wasn't exactly what she meant anyway. "We don't have to talk about this."

"You mean you don't *want* to talk about it."

Her hands trembled as she uncoiled lights. "We're supposed to be having a fun, festive family evening. Why ruin it with accusations that won't change anything that's happened?"

"You're right." He took his end of the lights toward

the outlet, the electric string stretched out between them. A second later, the entire strand began twinkling white in a cheery rhythm.

Rachel sat back on her heels. "Looks like they all work."

"Yeah. Guess there's nothing here I can fix." With that, he spun on his heel and left.

Which was only fair, she supposed. After all, she'd left him first.

DINNER did a lot more to restore Rachel's spirits than she would have guessed possible. She sat safely buffered between her father-in-law and Lilah. The bride-to-be chattered excitedly about her upcoming wedding. Everyone else was mostly free to nod and enjoy the home cooking. Susan's food was the old-fashioned, hearty kind that comforted the soul, carbs be damned.

When Arianne finished eating, she pushed away her plate and interrupted discussion of flowers, lace and music with a wicked grin. "You haven't mentioned the most important part—the bachelorette party!"

Tanner groaned.

Arianne ignored him. "Come on, Li. I'm the maid of honor. It's part of my job description. I wasn't even legally old enough to participate in the champagne toast when Rachel and David got married—you're not going to rob me of my fun now, are you? Besides, it will drive my brother crazy wondering what I have in store, and he picked on me a *lot* when I was younger."

Smacking a hand to his forehead, Tanner asked, "Would it help if I apologized for that now?"

"Not so much," Arianne said sweetly. She turned back to her friend. "You trust me, right?"

Lilah laughed knowingly. "Not even a little. Rach, you'll help Arianne with the party plans, won't you? Make sure she doesn't get too crazy."

"Oh, I don't know," Rachel heard herself say. "Maybe we could all use a crazy girls' night."

"Yes!" Arianne clapped her palms together. "Good to have you on board. Now, Lilah, you have a valid passport, right?"

Throughout the rest of the meal, Rachel and Arianne brainstormed facetious party ideas, each more outlandish than the last. If anyone noticed that David wasn't laughing quite as much as the rest of the family, no one drew attention to it. Clearing the table went quickly with so many helping hands, and they adjourned to the dining room, where the bare green Christmas tree waited.

"Aunt Shelby always popped popcorn to string on the tree," Lilah told them, "but Uncle Ray and I usually ate most of it."

Tanner lifted his hand to her lips, pressing a quick kiss across her knuckles. "Just think, soon we'll be able to start our own family traditions."

Susan glanced up from the piles she was making—sorting decorations by the room she planned to use them in—and smiled at Rachel. "How's your family doing, dear? They have big plans for the holidays?"

It occurred to Rachel then that her parents had never come to Mistletoe to see her for Christmas; they stayed in South Carolina to celebrate with Kate and her husband. It would have been nice if just once… Well. That hardly mattered now.

She cleared her throat. "Actually, I talked to my sister the other day, and she did have some big news. They're expecting their second child."

Even though Rachel kept her gaze locked on Susan and couldn't really see David's expression, she felt him tense, felt his sudden vibe of *oh, babe.* He would know more than anyone how deeply Kate's happy news had cut…and how disgusted Rachel was with herself because of that.

There was a flicker of what might have been pity in Susan's eyes, too, but she smiled brightly. "Your parents must be thrilled."

"Undoubtedly," Rachel said automatically. "You know, I have this craving for hot chocolate. Can I make some for everybody?"

She got several enthusiastic responses and promised extra marshmallows to Tanner before escaping the room. The pot of milk on the stove had barely begun to bubble when she heard footsteps behind her. *Oh, please let that be Arianne.* But she knew better.

"Thought I'd come see if you could use some help," her husband said.

Emotionally frayed, she snapped, "I'm perfectly capable of managing hot chocolate."

"Rachel." That was all, just her name and a wealth of understanding.

She slumped, feeling like a shrew. "I'm sorry." Being around David somehow brought out the worst in her. For that alone, she'd be eager to get out of Mistletoe. If she couldn't rediscover the person she'd once been, at least she could reshape herself into someone less wretched.

"You should have told me," he said. "About Kate."

Rachel smiled fondly. "And what would you have done?"

He was quiet for a moment, then smiled back. "Been extremely frustrated about the unfairness of life?"

The thing about David was that he believed he was a good listener. He meant well. But he liked *solving* problems and grew impatient when something didn't have a tidy solution. As their marriage went on, the problems between them had become more and more complex. And she'd turned to him less and less.

"I'm handling it okay," she lied, spooning cocoa into the mugs on the counter. "I just wasn't expecting it to come up tonight."

He crossed to the pantry and retrieved a bag of marshmallows. Then he was at her side, dumping a few into each cup. Rachel couldn't help breathing in his scent.

"You smell even better than the chocolate." Startled, she cast about for a way to take back the words.

"Thank you." David inclined his head, his expression unreadable. "My wife got me this cologne for my birthday."

Suddenly there was a hissing sound, and Rachel realized the milk was boiling over, a violent froth spilling from the pot. It would seem that she *was* incapable of making hot chocolate without help. Then again, it was her helper who'd distracted her in the first place.

David cleaned up the mess while she filled mugs. He carried the first batch into the next room. When she followed a few moments later, Tanner snapped his fingers, shaking his head at the archway she'd walked through.

"Another minute," he said, "and I would have had the mistletoe up. David could have caught you beneath it."

Arianne, wearing her long-suffering single-gal-surrounded-by-happy-couples expression, thumped him on the shoulder. "They're married, moron. He can kiss her anytime. This isn't like when you were courting Lilah and practically had to trick her into kissing you."

Lilah muffled a laugh and Tanner looked sheepish. It was no secret that he'd once screwed up their relationship and had to fight to win her back. *At least he thought she was* worth *fighting for.*

Rachel blinked, surprised by her melancholy. She should probably be *relieved* that David had accepted her decision so easily and hadn't made the separation even harder than it was.

From her position at the tree, Susan glanced at her. "Rachel, dear, we should have you take some pictures for us."

"If I can use your camera?" Rachel set her mug on a coaster. "I broke mine on Thanksgiving."

"Oh, that's right." Her mother-in-law frowned. "I'll have to dig mine out. I'd gotten so used to you being the family photographer—your pictures always turn out so well! Zachariah, do you know where our camera is?"

He retrieved it from a closet, handing it to Rachel with an expression of nearly boyish apology. "Afraid it's the old-fashioned kind that uses actual film. Places still develop that, don't they?"

She smiled. According to family stories, Zachariah hadn't always been the easiest father to live with, but he'd always been a big teddy bear with her. "Of course. Film is fine." The bigger problem was whether or not she could keep her hands from shaking with emotion.

It was on Thanksgiving, as she'd tried to set the automatic timer on her digital camera for a group shot, that she'd had the realization. Neither she nor David had truly been happy for weeks before that, possibly months, but neither of them were quitters. Neither of them had wanted to address the elephant in the room. But as she'd looked at the Waide family framed in the view window, it had struck her: *I don't belong here.* Seeing the way Lilah and Tanner smiled at each other, trying to recall just when she and David had stopped looking at each other that way, had hurt. Far worse had been watching David laugh at whatever teasing comment Arianne had been making. His face had been alive with humor and affection, such a contrast to the patient but shuttered expression he reserved for his wife.

She'd knocked over a seventy-dollar camera, but it had felt as if her world had crashed to the hardwood floor.

Well, she wasn't as fragile as a camera. As much as she hurt now, she had to believe she would heal eventually. Rachel threw herself into the tree-decorating, managing a smile at the many homemade, childish efforts. Even without glancing at the name on the back or the picture in some cases—such as Tanner's photo glued onto a green aluminum ashtray or Arianne's beaming smile, minus the top two teeth, framed in a construction of Popsicle sticks and spray-painted macaroni shells—Rachel could tell which Waide kid had made each decoration. Tanner was the one least likely to follow directions, which meant coloring outside the lines and in one instance, putting the ornament together upside down. Ari was the only one who'd used lace trim, pink buttons or little velvet bows. David's were exact. He must have been such a serious child, Rachel thought. Recalling how often she'd cringed at the prospect of disappointing her own parents, she wondered if the drive to succeed was simply part of the package for the firstborn.

Looking at his ornaments, one might think his personality consisted solely of careful measurements, straight lines and precision cutting. Those were certainly the aspects of himself he was most comfortable showing. She'd been the curved, crooked one in the relationship, the one whose body didn't even work with reliable precision.

"Whatcha got there?" Zachariah leaned over to see the ornament in Rachel's hand.

Holding it up by the ribbon, she showed him a laminated construction-paper star, each of its points equal to the others. Based on the year written in red permanent marker, David had probably been in first grade. "You guys have quite a collection."

Her father-in-law smiled affectionately. "I imagine it will grow even more when the grandkids start coming."

She couldn't help wincing.

Zachariah covered her hand with his own large, rough fingers. "More than one way to chase a dream, honey.

A few years ago, I wouldn't have realized that, too set in my ways. If you want to be a mama, it'll happen."

It was hard to speak around the lump in her throat, but she squeezed out a hoarse, "That's sweet."

"So who's going to put the star on top of the tree?" Tanner asked. "Obviously it needs to be someone taller than Ari. Even *with* the step stool, she'd barely reach."

His sister snorted. "Did I mention the really buff male dancers I'm planning for your wife's bachelorette party? Lilah, feel free to run off with Paolo rather than shackle yourself to this yahoo."

Ignoring the antics of his siblings, David asked, "How about you, Dad?"

"Or Lilah," Susan suggested. "To celebrate her joining the family."

Zachariah shook his head. "Rachel. She should do it." He didn't give a reason, but as head of the family, he didn't have to. Still, she was caught off guard by his choice. Did he know? Had he somehow guessed that she wouldn't be here next year, that this was her goodbye?

He took the small box from his wife and extracted the shining gold ornament. "Here. You know what they say about stars. Make a wish."

Make a wish? She wouldn't know where to begin. But as she scooted the stool toward the tree and climbed onto it, her gaze met David's. The obvious big wish was how much she'd wanted to be a mommy. If she had it all to do it again, though, there were so many small moments where she wished she'd made different decisions, tiny moments in a couple's life that moved them apart so subtly that they hadn't even realized it until they were staring at each other from different shores.

Rachel was afraid a single star couldn't help her. She needed a galaxy or, barring that, a fresh start.

Chapter Five

Rachel parked the car, then sat staring into the gray morning light. *You are going to feel like an idiot if you do this.* Technically she felt like one already, driving to the store this early on what felt like a fool's errand. But it was Saturday; she still hadn't started her period. What if—?

Stop it. Too many times she'd allowed the painful blade of hope to slip beneath her ribs. She was here simply to rule out the unlikely possibility so that she could stop torturing herself. Huddling deeper into her hooded knit sweater, she opened her door. As she hurried toward the grocery store, it occurred to her that there were more cars in the lot than she would have expected on an overcast weekend morning. With temperatures dropping and rain in the forecast, this was the perfect kind of day for sleeping in—a luxurious concept that Winnie's dogs did not grasp. Rachel had quickly learned that it was folly to ignore the whimpering of a puppy who hadn't been outside yet.

The store's automatic doors parted, and she sighed at the immediate warm air. On mornings like these, she couldn't imagine why anyone willingly lived up north.

Inside, she faltered, not entirely ready to know the truth one way or the other. Stalling, she grabbed a cart even though she only intended to buy one thing. When the test came up negative, it would close another chapter on her marriage—necessary but painful. *Like a root canal.*

She squared her shoulders and shoved the cart, its one squeaky wheel grating a resolute tattoo against the tile. The pharmacy section was just ahead. Determined to get this over with, she rounded the corner at top speed, nearly crashing into Mindy Nelson.

"Sorry." Rachel drew up short. The older woman had her buggy parked directly in front of the section Rachel needed.

"Hi! Haven't seen you around much lately." Following Rachel's gaze, Mindy arched an eyebrow. "Am I in your way, hon?"

Since there was nothing on the other side of the woman but pregnancy tests, Rachel shook her head in quick denial. "No. I was just on this aisle to get some…lotion." Blindly she grabbed a container off the shelf closest to her.

"Well, I'm glad I ran into you. You'll be buying tickets to the winter dance this year, won't you?" Mindy was one of the administrative staff at the local seniors' center. Every year they sponsored a charity ball held at the Mistletoe Inn to benefit the center.

"Sure, put me down for one," Rachel said distractedly. Even if she didn't attend, she was happy to make the donation.

"Don't you mean two?"

"What?" Nervously she grabbed another tube to give her hands something to do. "Oh, two tickets. Of course.

My brain's not really awake yet. Winnie's dogs have been getting me up early, so I'm on autopilot for most of the morning."

"I see." Mindy peered into Rachel's cart, making her aware that she'd thoughtlessly accumulated four bottles of lotion.

"My skin gets so dry during the winter," Rachel babbled. *Go away, go away!*

"Uh-huh. Well, you take care. And tell that dishy husband of yours I said hello. I look forward to seeing you both at the dance."

"Right. Bye now."

Finally, Mindy returned to her cart and leisurely steered it to the next aisle. Rachel waited another moment, her palms sweaty and her heart thudding. One of the boxes announced in boldfaced type: Now you can know two days *before* your missed period! She was waaay past that. Taking a deep breath, she grabbed the box and tossed it into the buggy. It bounced off one of the lotion bottles.

Sighing, she gathered the bottles up and began placing them back on the shelf. Then she headed in the direction of the checkout lanes. She wasn't sure exactly what she noticed as she walked by the shampoo aisle, what she glanced in her peripheral vision that left her rooted to the spot. *David.* Was he so familiar, imprinted on her brain, that she knew him even with the barest sidelong glimpse? Maybe she'd instinctively recognized his jacket, which she had given him. Or smelled his familiar soap-shampoo combination. Whatever tipped her off, she took comfort in the fact that *he* hadn't noticed *her* yet. She had her hood up; maybe she could just—

"Rachel?"

She scrambled around the side of the cart, retrieving the lone item inside and trying to tuck it beneath the hem of her sweater before he noticed. After the holidays, she needed to think seriously about making her fresh start somewhere else, not a small Georgia town that had only one major grocery store. "Hi."

"You're out and about early," he said casually. "You looked so tired when you left Mom and Dad's last night, I expected you would sleep late."

The same frantic dizziness she'd felt in the car last week overcame her, a hundred times worse. She willed it away. David would probably notice if she hyperventilated or—

"Miss!" A man in a white shirt and red pharmacy vest was speed-walking down the aisle, waving his hands. "Miss, I'm afraid I need to... Oh, hi, Mrs. Waide."

Rachel had refilled enough prescriptions here that most of the pharmacy staff knew her by name.

The bespectacled young man gestured at her hood. "I didn't realize it was you. Thought you were a shoplifter."

David laughed outright. "A shoplifter? She once made me turn around and drive back into Atlanta when she realized the restaurant left our dessert off the bill."

"Well, I was afraid it would come out of the waiter's pay," she said weakly.

Too bad she didn't have that Christmas-tree star with her now; she knew *exactly* what she'd wish for—the earth to open up and swallow her whole before the kid in the vest—

"Well, obviously *she's* not a shoplifter. But you

wouldn't believe what people are too embarrassed to buy from this section. When she stuck that box under her—"

"I was on my way to pay for it!" She flinched at the shrillness of her own voice. The pharmacy guy actually rubbed his ear.

David pinned her with his gaze. "What box?"

"Nothing. Girl stuff," she prevaricated, already walking toward the register.

Her stubborn husband, holding his green basket of skim milk and men's deodorant, fell in step with her. "You're embarrassed? Hell, Rach, I've bought tampons for you before."

"That was different."

"You know, you should probably put the 'girl stuff,'" he said in an exaggerated whisper, "in the cart so that no one else thinks you're shoplifting."

"No one else saw me with it." But when David chose to pursue something, he was doggedly single-minded. It would be just like him to follow her into the line. She chunked the pregnancy test back into the cart.

His jaw dropped. For a moment, she took satisfaction in having rendered him speechless.

"When," he demanded, "were you going to tell me?"

"I don't even know if there's anything *to* tell. Hence, the test."

His blue eyes shone. "You think there's a chance, though?"

He looked excited, and it was hard to battle back her own automatic eagerness. A baby! What would it be like to hold a baby of her own? She gave a little jerk of her head. *Don't set yourself up for disappointments.*

"I don't know," she said.

"You'd have to be more than a month and a half along. Maybe two?" In his enthusiasm, he was getting louder, drawing a few glances. "It's been at least that long since—"

"Hey! Do you mind if we don't have this conversation in the middle of the grocery store?"

"Good point. I'll follow you to Winnie's," he said decisively. "Unless you want to come home?"

No, she had the memory of too many tests there, too many broken-hearted moments. "David, this could be nothing. It's *probably* nothing. I can call you later. Or we could have lunch?" That would give her time to adjust either way.

He stared. "You've got to be joking. After everything we went through to…"

You mean everything I went through? It was a knee-jerk reaction. She knew it wasn't fair. The physical side effects, and a significant portion of the emotional ones, had been hers to bear, but he'd paid his own price for their attempts.

"All right," she conceded. "I'll wait for you at Winnie's."

She barely allowed herself to peek at her rearview mirror on the drive to their subdivision, but she exhaled in relief as she approached Winnie's house. David wasn't behind her yet, so she had a few minutes to get her rioting emotions under control. She'd wanted this so badly, for so long, that hope seemed a natural response. But the timing! Divorce in the middle of a pregnancy? There was fear, too, as she relived the pains that had awakened her in the spring, the sight of blood and the sudden, excruciating knowledge that she and David wouldn't be parents by winter after all.

With the back of her hand, she dashed away a few tears. Even from the driveway, she could hear the dogs barking in greeting. It was best not to leave Hildie inside when she got excited. Besides, the dogs would pitch a fit when David showed up, and Rachel could do without the clamor. Her temples were throbbing.

By the time David arrived, she'd ushered the dogs into the yard and poured two glasses of tea. It felt strangely formal and a little surreal, her own husband knocking on the front door. She thought briefly of their first date, the way her pulse had jumped when he'd knocked on the door of her hotel room. She'd told him when he asked her to dinner that she wouldn't be in town long. *Then you should* definitely *have dinner with me,* he'd said, undeterred. *It's a limited-time opportunity.* He'd been so good-looking.

He still was. The difference was that, back then, she'd delighted in being swept off her feet with no thought for what would happen once she landed.

In the kitchen, she handed him a glass. "Sorry it's so sweet. I wasn't expecting you when I brewed it." David liked his iced tea with barely enough sugar to still call himself a Southerner.

"Thank you." He studied her face as if searching for clues. Was he trying to decide if she looked pregnant?

"Or there might be some soda left in the fridge," she said nervously.

"Rach, I didn't come over for the drink."

She gripped the back of a kitchen chair. "I know that. I'm just…"

"Anxious?" He smiled gently.

"Petrified. You?" In this candid moment in an acquaintance's kitchen, Rachel felt closer to him than she had during the past three months in their own house. An unspoken truce sheltered them as they teetered on the edge of discovery.

"I'm not sure," he admitted.

She returned his smile. "David Waide is unsure of something? *The* David Waide?"

"Yeah, well, we'll call that big surprise number *two* of the morning." He glanced pointedly at the white plastic grocery bag on the counter.

She tucked a lock of hair behind her ear. "You know that if it turns out…if it had turned out positive, I never would have kept it from you. There didn't seem like anything to tell yet. I was still—"

"I get it." He set his untouched drink on the table. "So."

Right. The moment of truth. "Why don't you, uh, have a seat, and I'll be right back?"

"Okay." He swallowed. "Rach…"

She looked back over her shoulder.

"I don't know. I feel like I should say something." He flashed a wan smile. "Good luck?"

A semihysterical laugh burbled out of her. Once upon a time, the only thing she'd ever worried about before a test was whether her parents would be satisfied with an A, in case she fell short of an A-plus.

She thoroughly read the instructions, even though she'd done this before. After completing the necessary tasks, she decided to rejoin David. Even with the strain between them, she didn't want to wait by herself for the next three minutes. He was pacing restlessly, but halted when he saw her. The question burned bright in his eyes.

"We're supposed to wait now," she explained.

"Oh. How long?"

She glanced at the clock on the microwave. "Probably two more minutes."

"Ah." He resumed pacing.

"That's not helping my nerves," she said without hostility.

"Actually, it's not doing much to calm mine, either." He stopped in midlap, on the opposite side of the kitchen island from her.

Winnie's floor plan was so similar to theirs that Rachel could easily envision her own copper-bottom pots hanging above them, could practically hear the ticking of the cuckoo clock they'd bought during a weekend getaway in Helen, Georgia.

Finding yourself on a blind date with a first cousin was probably less awkward than this. "How's the store doing?" she asked.

"Good. You know we hired Chloe to do a Web site? We've already filled our first out-of-state orders." He sounded understandably proud. The supply store had been in the family for generations, and it was still improving and growing. All the Waides were involved to some extent, even Tanner, who ran an independent bookkeeping business.

Had David planned on raising their own child to take a hand in the business?

She considered the hypothetical. If it were up to her, she'd encourage the kid to go see more of the world before deciding to settle here. Mistletoe was a lovely community but insulated. Set in its ways. If you didn't already have an idea of who you were and what you wanted, you might not figure it out here. Instead, you fell into a role other people defined for you. David had put in a good word for her and she'd easily snagged the job with May before their wedding, but she'd never intended to be there five years later. First enjoying the reduced workload and life as a newlywed, later focused on trying to start a family, she'd let her career aspirations fall away. Now there was a distinctly empty place in her life.

She'd made major decisions at a time when she was upset about her father's health and uncertain about her own future—moving here, abandoning her career...marrying David. The result was that she'd leaned too much on him and the people she'd met in Mistletoe, too much on their hopes of having a baby. David had seemed to her as chivalrous as a medieval knight rescuing a damsel in distress. He wasn't to blame for her realization that she didn't want to *be* that damsel. He showed his love by coddling, and she was tired of being smothered. He expressed affection by anticipating her needs, and she was tired of someone making decisions for her. Whenever she'd gently tried to protest, he'd been confused and she'd felt ungrateful. Wouldn't he be better off with someone who fully appreciated his gallantry?

David cleared his throat. "It's been two minutes. Do you want me to wait here?" There was that underlying uncertainty in his voice again; it touched her in a way his overbearing confidence never could.

"Why don't you come with me?" she offered.

Together, they padded silently down the hall. Outside the bathroom, David reached for her hand. She didn't pull away.

But she did jerk to a stop inches shy of the threshold. "I can't look. You do it."

"You sure?"

She just couldn't. Given the timing, it would probably be for the best if she weren't pregnant, but emotionally, she couldn't face another negative response. "I'm sure. It's sitting next to the sink."

Closing her eyes, she waited an interminable heartbeat of time, heard him suck in his breath.

"Oh my God." His words were a reverent whisper.

"You're kidding!" She knew he'd never joke about this. Still, maybe he'd misread the test, or… "Let me see."

He moved aside, letting out an earsplitting whoop even as she viewed the proof for herself. "We're pregnant!"

Her knees trembled at the sight of the pink plus sign. *I'm pregnant?*

I'm pregnant! She was carrying David's baby. Tears welled in her eyes. Before she could classify them as happy crying or something more bittersweet, David pulled her into his strong arms.

And kissed her.

It caught Rachel totally off guard since she'd anticipated a hug of support or mutual joy. But he lowered his dark head, his intent registering a fraction of a second before his lips brushed hers. Hunger ignited deep inside her, flaring an excitement through her body that was startling in its force. After all, she'd kissed this man hundreds of times, the last dozen of which had felt rather obligatory.

This, though. Even knowing it was a mistake, she couldn't help parting her mouth, tangling her arms around him and leaning into his warmth. He stroked his tongue against hers, drew back and sucked lightly at her bottom lip. A moan rippled through her. Her already unsteady legs threatened to give out from under her.

She would have liked to think self-discipline gave her the strength to pull away, but actually it was the realization that she could easily lose her balance. The two of them toppling over and cracking their skulls on Winnie's bathtub was not how she wanted to commemorate the moment.

"W-wait." She angled her head away, her voice breathless. *"Wait."*

"Right," he said sharply. His arms still around her, he maneuvered them into the hallway and began kissing her again.

Oh, she'd missed this. Missed feeling desire, missed feeling desirable. She thrust her tongue into his mouth, bunching his shirt in her hands. It wasn't easy to move, pressed as she was between his hard body and the wall at her back, but she didn't mind. The way their bodies slid together merely fueled her longing. When David's hand slipped down the curve of her neck to the slope of her breast, she arched into his palm. But as he began to push aside the fabric of her shirt, reality clanged a warning bell in her head.

What the hell am I doing? She wasn't sure, but it felt great. *Not the point!*

"David? Mmm...David, I—" She tilted her head back, closing her eyes as he kissed the exposed line of her throat. "David!"

He straightened, his expression dazed. Under other circumstances, she would have smiled at that. "Guess we shouldn't be doing this at Winnie's house?"

Men truly were from another planet. "We shouldn't be doing this *at all!*" While he was still motionless, she took the opportunity to duck under his arm and scamper away. They needed distance.

"Rachel, you can't mean it." His normal composure was already falling back into place. "You wanted me as much as I want you."

Well, she couldn't argue that. "It's true I was caught up in the moment, but temporary insanity aside, it would be a mistake for us to..." Have wild, passionate sex, the kind that had been the hallmark of their honeymoon? "...do anything physical. We're *separated.*" Even as she said the word, a pang of loss assailed her.

"We *were* separated." He held his hands palms up, gesturing toward her abdomen. "This changes everything."

His presumption would have been annoying if she hadn't been kissing him fervently ten seconds ago. She could see where that was a mixed signal. "My being pregnant complicates things," she said gently, "but it doesn't necessarily change anything."

In the last year, angry at her infertile body and feeling she'd settled into a dead-end job, her self-esteem had taken a bit of a beating, something she was determined to correct. But what would it do to her pride to walk back to a man who'd seemed content to let her go just because she was having his child? While she understood the theory of staying together for kids, parenthood brought with it plenty of stress. You didn't try to build houses on cracked foundations.

"The hell it doesn't change things." He looked more bewildered than angry. "Rach, you're having my baby! I know you were upset because you couldn't get pregnant, but…"

Upset hardly seemed adequate for what she'd endured emotionally and physically.

"That wasn't the only problem," she reminded him quietly. "And…I *hope* I'm having a baby. We both know that just because you conceive—" She couldn't bring herself to finish the horrible thought.

"Oh, babe. Stop. Don't even let yourself go there. C'mere." He cradled her head against his chest. "Let me be there for you. You shouldn't go through this all alone. You don't want the tribulations of being a single mother."

Not *I love you, Rach, I miss you,* only *You can't do this by yourself, you need me.* She straightened. "I'm glad you were here, David. I really am, but it's time you leave."

"You're mad." He studied her with a blend of puzzlement and martyrlike patience. She didn't know which aggravated her more. "You left, but I'm here trying to help and somehow *you're* angry with *me?* Maybe it's hormones making you emotional, but—"

"It's not the hormones," she interrupted before he angered her any further. At least, she amended silently, it wasn't *just* the hormones. Part of it was repression. When she was upset or angry, he tried to tell her why she was wrong. When she was scared or worried, instead of hearing out her concerns, he told her not to entertain negative thoughts. Over time, she'd built up a volcano's worth of emotions that had blown shortly after Thanksgiving. "Please go. We have Lilah's shower this afternoon, and I have a lot to sort through before then."

"I'll help," he said promptly.

"You're doing it again." She tried to keep the exasperation out of her voice, but wasn't entirely successful. "You think you're listening to me, but you're not *hearing* me. The best help you can give me right now is to leave me alone. Why do you always somehow think you know what I need better than I do?"

"That's not fair." He drew back, indignant. "When I met you, you were trying to figure out what you needed. You were overworked, overstressed, looking for a life change. I was there for you."

"Yes, you were." Which was how she'd ended up walking away from the career and home she'd been building and straight into Mistletoe, where his life had been mapped out since birth. "David, I will always be grateful to you for helping me through a bad time, but the situation's changed. *I've* changed. I'm not looking for someone to rescue me."

He said nothing, but the muscle tic in his jaw suggested that he wasn't mollified by her words.

She took deep breaths. Whatever else was between them, she'd loved this man with all her heart—still loved him, on some level. And the possibility of this baby was a miracle. Having his child would bind her to David forever, even if their marriage vows failed to do so. The last thing she wanted was a future of bitter enmity between them.

"It's okay," she relented. "You had good intentions. And maybe you're right about the hormones exaggerating everything I'm feeling right now. I don't want to fight."

"Me, either." He ducked his head guiltily. "That can't be good for the baby. Dr. McDermott would kick my butt. You'll let me go with you, won't you? To the doctor's?"

"Of course. I want you to have an equal part in this." That's what she'd always wanted—equal partnership—though he'd always been affronted when she tried to explain.

"All right. Then I'll go so that you can get some rest before the shower." He smoothed her hair. "But I'm just down the street if you need anything or have any cravings or—"

"David." She shook her head. "I'll be fine. But if I need anything, I know how to find you."

After he left, she leaned against the front door and pressed a finger to her still-tingling lips. Kissing him had been amazing. She couldn't help imagining, just for a second, what it would have been like to allow herself the indulgence of being swept away, of making love to him again. *And then what?* She'd meant what she said; the infertility issues had no doubt exacerbated their problems, exposing the fault lines of their marriage, but they hadn't been why she left.

It was true that she'd never planned to be a single mom, but nor did she plan to slap this pregnancy over their marriage like a Band-Aid. David had barely protested when she'd told him the marriage was over. She knew her husband. If he'd wanted to fight for her, nothing on earth would have stopped him. Fighting for the baby, while understandable, was not the same thing. Marriage wasn't a cracked Christmas ornament. He couldn't glue it back together, hang it on the tree and pretend everything was okay.

Chapter Six

The couples' shower for Tanner and Lilah was being hosted by Sandra Donavan, one of the other teachers at Whiteberry Elementary, and her husband, Pat. Rachel had never been to their house before, but the giant white bell-shaped balloon tied to the mailbox outside made it easy to find. What was a bit more difficult to find was parking—a line of cars had already formed halfway up the street. Rachel climbed out of the car, bracing herself against the freezing rain, and locked her doors, even though she didn't know the last time anything was stolen in Mistletoe.

She carried her purse, umbrella and a plastic-wrapped platter with enough ham-and-cheese-melt mini-sandwiches for fourteen guests. It was a good thing David was bringing the gift from the two of them since she didn't have a free hand.

"Hey."

At the sound of David's voice, she turned on the sidewalk. "I was just thinking about you," she blurted. She glanced at the silver-wrapped package in his hands. "I mean, about the fact that you were bringing the present."

A lot of people, herself included, relied on cute gift bags. Not David. He hand-wrapped everything with precision corners and perfectly coordinated ribbons.

Out of nowhere, a burble of laughter escaped her. "It's a good thing you're so secure in your masculinity."

"Less secure by the hour." He fell in step with her, but remained on the street since their open umbrellas didn't allow for their walking abreast on the sidewalk. "Just earlier today, I was shot down by a beautiful woman."

Beautiful? Not sure how to respond, she concentrated on getting out of the rain quickly.

Rachel tried not to think about how many women in town would line up to console him once their separation was public knowledge. Ladies had sought her out at council meetings and softball games to tell her just how lucky she was. A few of them had sounded a bit jealous, miffed that one of Mistletoe's most eligible bachelors had chosen an outsider, but most had simply been sincere. She thought again of how she would miss the people when she left, what Mistletoe had meant to her when she first visited.

My sanctuary. She'd come to this quaint town on vacation, after her dad had been released from the hospital. She'd worried that he was working himself to death…and was disturbed by the possibility that she was headed down the same sixty-hour-a-week path in a career she'd never consciously sought. She'd always let whatever classes she was getting the highest grades in determine her course, shaping her major and eventually her internship with a marketing firm in Columbia. But there'd never been a moment when she'd sat down, thought it out, and said, "Aha! This is what I want to be when I grow up."

So she'd taken some personal time from work, hiking in North Georgia, taking scads of pictures and letting herself be charmed by small-town citizens. One in particular. She'd warned David that her time here was temporary and that she wasn't interested in a brief fling, yet she'd dated him anyway. Guided by his vision of the future, she'd suddenly been able to see what she wanted, her nebulous plans crystallized into brilliant focus. David had made it seem so matter-of-fact; she would move here, be with him. They would raise a family and be deliriously happy, end of story. For a woman who had always obligingly gone with the flow, pleasing people around her and ignoring any selfish impulses, it had been intoxicating to consider such a bold move. After a few months of long-distance dating, they'd wound up engaged and she'd moved here exactly as he'd outlined. For a little while, they *had* been deliriously happy.

Now that they were apart, she'd known she couldn't bear to stay in Mistletoe. It was too small—there wasn't enough room for her, her ex and five years of accumulated memories. But then, she hadn't counted on parenting from two different zip codes. She had to figure out a life plan that was good for their baby without jeopardizing her own sanity or further damaging her heart. David had had a point this morning; the pregnancy *did* change things. She just had to figure out which things and how much.

Turning, she headed up the sidewalk, glad that she and David were arriving together so that she didn't babble through another explanation of why they'd taken two separate cars. Sandra opened the door, calling out a cheerful hello. As they stepped inside the two-story stone-and-wood house, each wiping their feet on the entry mat, Sandra looked back out the glass door.

"Heck of a day we picked to have a party, huh?"

Rachel handed over her tray of sandwiches. "At least you weren't planning to do this in the backyard."

"I've cooked out in worse weather," her husband, Pat, said as he came into the foyer to greet them.

Rolling her eyes, Sandra laughed. "My husband thinks of barbecuing as an extreme sport."

Pat mock-glared. "Never heard you complain while eating my award-winning brisket." He reached out and squeezed her shoulder, both of them grinning.

Rachel's throat constricted—it was just the teasing by-play of two people in love who were comfortable with each other, but it was easy to take for granted until you lost it. She and David hadn't been comfortable in months; they'd become as hard and fragile as peanut brittle.

"Rachel, David." Lilah appeared in the archway behind their hosts. "You guys made it! We're just waiting on Amy and Steve."

Steve played on Tanner's softball team, and his wife, Amy, worked in the administration office of the elementary school. Gathered inside the Donavans' living room already were Lilah's aunt Shelby and uncle Ray, Vonda Kerrigan and her white-haired boyfriend Peter Joel and Quinn and Ari, who'd jokingly agreed to be each other's dates since neither of them was currently seeing anyone special. Susan and Zachariah Waide had also been

invited, but they were working at the store so their
children could all attend. The Christmas season was the
busiest time of year in retail.

The party kicked off the way most did in Mistletoe, with
small talk while the guests piled their plates with food.

"You sit down. I'll bring you something," David in-
structed Rachel, gesturing toward the mismatched furniture. The Donavans had an adjoining dining room and
living room that worked to create one large space; obviously they'd dragged chairs and even a love seat from
other areas to accommodate the large number of guests.

She took a spot on a padded bench next to Arianne. The
two of them were chatting about some upcoming holiday
movies when Rachel realized her husband had returned.

"Thank y— Good heavens." Rachel stared, trying to
decide if this was his idea of a joke.

Even Arianne blinked. "Is that for Rachel and I to
share? She can't possibly eat all that."

David glanced at the plate that was threatening to
bow under the weight of the food he'd heaped on it. "It's
not *that*... Okay, maybe I got carried away. But—"

"But what?" Arianne asked.

But I'm eating for two now? Was that what David had
been thinking? A silly old-time cliché that was hardly applicable in her case since the baby was probably the size
of a small lima bean. *The baby.* Rachel found herself
grinning foolishly. Lima bean or not, it was still her baby.

"Rach? David? One of you going to tell me why
you're behaving so strangely?"

"Nothing strange," Rachel said, her voice breathy.
Miraculous, wondrous, unexpected, but not strange. "I

just…haven't had a chance to eat today. Got caught up in that special scrapbooking project, and David's trying to look out for me."

"Which my wife," David intoned, "does not always have the good sense to appreciate."

She shot him a warning look. "Maybe I'd appreciate it if you trusted me to look out for myself. I might even appreciate looking out for someone else, not that you ever seem to need it."

He frowned, bemused. "So, what, you're upset that I'm self-sufficient and successful? I thought women *looked* for stuff like that in mates. I married a crazy woman."

"Ummm." Arianne stood. "I think I'm just gonna go hang out with Vonda." She crossed the room to where the feisty septuagenarian was entertaining people with tall tales about her father and uncles trying unsuccessfully to brew their own alcohol during Prohibition.

Gesturing toward the spot his sister had just vacated and looking somewhat abashed, David asked, "Mind if I sit there?"

A little, but it wasn't as if she could make him sit on the floor without it appearing weird. Then again, he'd just called her crazy so maybe she was entitled. "Suit yourself." They still had a number of prenuptial festivities, a family Christmas and the wedding itself to get through—she could be mature about this. Even if being so close to David exasperated her, aroused her and made her want to cry all at the same time. *He's right. I am a little crazy.*

Amy and Steve arrived a few minutes later, and guests went back for second helpings. Thirds, in the case of a few of the guys. Once everyone was stuffed, Amy declared that it was time for the Soon-to-be-Newlywed game and passed out little pads of paper and pencils so that everyone could write down their answers.

Tanner leaned over to Lilah and loudly whispered, "No one told me there would be a quiz!"

She laughed. "You sound like my students."

Amy explained that she was going to ask each couple the same questions and they would jot down a response, then compare at the end to see which pair had the highest number of matches.

Arianne smirked at Quinn from her folding chair across the room. "How awesome would it be if we won?"

Lilah laughed again. "I'm pretty sure I'd be traumatized to learn that two of my bridesmaids are more compatible than my husband and I."

"We playin' for money?" Vonda wanted to know.

Amy shook her head. "Just gloating rights."

"That works, too," Vonda said gleefully.

The first question was, Where did you meet? Rachel thought back to the diner where she'd seen David, the memory so vivid she could smell chicken-fried steak cooking. His smile had been bright enough she could practically sunbathe in it. The second question, What's your song? was more difficult.

She frowned. "What if you don't have one?"

"Make something up," Arianne called back. "That's what I'm doing."

Lilah giggled. "You're both lucky. I first fell for Tanner in the era of boy bands and mix tapes. What seemed soulful to me then now seems cheesy enough to serve on crackers."

"Hey!" Tanner glanced up from his pad of paper, looking offended.

Lilah kissed his cheek. "But I like cheese."

Rachel continued staring at her own piece of paper. She and David hadn't dated long enough to go through the courtship rites of stuff like mix tapes. Everything for them had happened quickly. Except getting pregnant. She knew girlfriends in college defined a couple's song by what had been playing on the radio the first time they had sex, but there hadn't been music on in the background when she and David made love. It had been at his old apartment, on a rainy afternoon.

In a whisper so faint even she could barely hear it, David murmured, "'Raindrops Keep Fallin' on My Head'?"

Rachel blushed. Somehow knowing that they were both reliving the same interlude was nearly as intimate as the act itself had been.

"Hey," Steve objected from the other side of the room. "No signaling partners over there."

Next they had to remember when they last kissed each other. Rachel warmed at the memory of this morning, pressed against the wall of Winnie's hallway, feeling her body come back to erotic life after numbingly frustrating months of hibernation.

"Can Ari and I be excused from this one?" Quinn asked wryly.

While everyone was chuckling, Rachel stood. "I, ah, just need to borrow your restroom, Sandra, but you guys go ahead and play without me. I'm happy to let someone else win the gloating rights."

David narrowed his eyes at her. "Quitter." His tone was light, but she read a wealth of accusation into it.

Had she been wrong to leave? It had seemed so agonizingly clear at the time, but in the wake of this morning's news and the flood of memories this afternoon, Rachel was confused. She knew that she and David had loved each other, but she also knew that they had problems, not a misunderstanding over whether one of them had flirted with someone else or an argument because one of them never put their socks in the hamper. Could they meet each other's emotional needs without hurting each other?

Still, it was seductive, the *what if?* that whispered in her ear as she watched Lilah open presents later that afternoon. Sandra had repeated the old wives' tale that the number of ribbons the bride broke foretold the number of children the newlyweds would eventually have. At the mention of babies, Rachel found herself unconsciously rubbing her abdomen. If David gave her time and space to figure out what she wanted, *if* he could truly hear her perspective and understand it, could this be them in seven or eight months? Surrounded by friends, grinning at each other, eating off pink and blue plates with booties printed on them instead of pale gold plates with interlocking rings?

She just didn't know. If David really thought she was a crazy quitter who got overemotional and didn't appreciate what a good thing he'd had…well, then, no wonder he hadn't fought to save their marriage.

Chapter Seven

Just going for a run, nothing more. Definitely not stalking. The rationalization had seemed more convincing in the foyer of his own house as David laced up his running shoes Monday morning. After all, he went jogging at least three times a week. No ulterior motives there. Of course, he didn't normally go in an endless loop up and down Winnie's street, hoping for a glimpse of his wife.

Was she still sleeping, like most of the neighborhood, or had the dogs already awakened her? Was she experiencing nausea? Rachel *hated* to throw up. He supposed everyone did, but she'd fought it during the flu and one bout of food poisoning when he'd reminded her she'd feel better if she just got it over with. He wished he could bring her a cold cloth or glass of water or something.

David hated feeling useless, helpless. The way he'd felt for nearly a year.

It had been so frustrating watching his wife slip away, becoming practically a stranger. Once upon a time, they'd tackled problems together. Since the miscarriage, everything had changed. If he could have suffered it for her or shielded her from that loss... But there'd been nothing he could do. She'd seemed so unreachable, and he'd felt angry and impotent. Eventually she'd suggested they try again, she'd started smiling on a daily basis and, although most people assumed she was all right, she hadn't been the same. After being so frustrated at being shut out, neither had he.

David had wondered if what they were doing—the medical appointments, the physical side effects of the treatment, the emotional and financial cost—was worth it. He and Rachel had a lot of love to give and it seemed as if adoption would be so much easier. When he'd told her that, she'd distanced herself even more. Her emotional rebuffs had infuriated him, reducing him to a glorified sperm donor. She couldn't talk to him, couldn't lean on him anymore, but she could expect him to jump into her bed when the ovulation kits said it was time?

Pride. Was he really going to throw away a life with the woman he loved just because she'd hurt his feelings?

He'd handled this all wrong. When she'd told him their marriage was faltering, that she didn't think she could do this anymore, he'd honestly thought some distance might be good for both of them. Deep down, though, he'd never accepted it as the end. He'd believed—just thinking it made him feel petty, but Rachel's absence was forcing some hard truths—he'd believed she would see how much she needed him, that she'd blamed him for things that weren't his fault and would come home. He would forgive her, wait a respectable period of time, then try to persuade her to pursue the reasonable course of adoption.

Her walking out had hurt his male ego, stunting his emotional response. Other than snapping at her once or twice, he'd barely *had* a response. How much time did he have to repair his mistakes—nine months? Less.

There was a light on in Winnie's house now, and he stared at it, hoping no one mistook him for a prowler. What if he didn't have until the baby was born but only a matter of *weeks?* Would Rachel follow through on her plan to leave after the wedding? What if she didn't intend to have the baby in Mistletoe?

David's heart raced, and it had nothing to do with his so-called run. Pure, unadulterated panic coursed through his veins. *I have to get them back.* She'd fallen in love with a take-charge guy who'd taken one look at her and set about wooing her. He was still that man.

And he refused to lose his wife.

"Whoa." May let out a low whistle as she glanced from the front door to Rachel, who was installing a new ink cartridge in one of their printers. "Since I haven't had a hot date in months, I'm guessing those are for you."

"Guessing *what* are for me?" Rachel asked cautiously.

"Half of Natalie's shop, by the looks of it."

Former Mistletoe High cheerleader Natalie Young was the majority owner of the local flower shop and in charge of floral arrangements for Tanner and Lilah's wedding. Someone had sent flowers? Rachel left the printer and joined her co-worker at the counter. *Whoa* didn't begin to cover it.

"Delivery for Rachel Waide." The cheerful delivery boy was barely visible behind the profusion of pink roses, white tulips and smaller graceful yellow flowers, all arranged with greenery in a crystal vase that probably weighed a ton.

May was practically vibrating with excitement. "That's her! She's Rachel."

While Rachel stood frozen in shock, the other two settled the flowers atop the counter. May nudged her.

"I think you're supposed to sign for them."

David. A guy didn't send his estranged wife flowers, did he?

Then again, maybe she was reading too much into this. Maybe he was simply excited over their news. She'd been so awestruck that, even though she'd felt bone-tired, she hadn't been able to sleep. She'd spent the night awake, staring at the ceiling, wondering how many months before she could feel the baby move, day-dreaming about nursery themes and a little girl with David's blue eyes or a little boy with his smile.

Her doctor's appointment was tomorrow afternoon; she'd e-mailed David with the time and suggested they meet there. This bouquet was probably a platonic expression of joy. She plucked the card from the plastic holder in the center of the flowers. He'd written the note himself; she knew his handwriting as well as she knew her own.

Congratulations! I'm sorry I couldn't find flowers as beautiful as you are, but I hope this paltry offering will still demonstrate how happy I am. (I'd be even happier if you came home.)
Love, Your Husband

"Do I get to read it?" May asked, unrepentantly nosy.

"It's personal." And inappropriate. It was impossible to let David off on the platonic-joy defense if he was going to sling around words like *beautiful* and *your husband*.

"Okay, I get that it's personal," May conceded. "But we're friends. You could tell me anything in confidence. You know that, right?"

"Like what?" Rachel was a little taken aback by the intense, meaningful glances her boss was giving her. Since no one knew about the separation, her husband sending flowers wasn't *that* notable. He'd done so once or twice on special occasions. "I'm not having a steamy affair with Paolo or anything."

May's eyebrows shot upward. "Who's Paolo?"

"Nothing, nobody. Imaginary male stripper." She needed to call Arianne back about the bachelorette party. "I just meant, the flowers are from David."

"To celebrate a happy event, maybe? Or a happy future event you're *expecting?*"

How does she know? Rachel's bewilderment and her tacit admission must both be readable in her expression because May laughed.

"Oh, honey. When I walked in here last week with that fish sandwich, you turned positively green. And Mindy Nelson saw you in the women's aisle at the grocery store. She said you were acting nutty. We've both had our fingers crossed for you all weekend."

Perhaps the conjecture had been unavoidable, but Rachel wished David hadn't cemented the gossip with flowers. She was still in the statistically dangerous first tri-mester. One of the worst parts of the miscarriage had been running into people who somehow hadn't heard the news yet, having to suffer through the painful well-meaning questions and the awkward strain once she told them.

"Don't get too excited just yet," Rachel warned.

But her words seemed to have the opposite effect on May, whose eyes brightened. "So you do at least *think* you're pregnant?"

"I don't know for sure. Even if I am, I'm not ready to tell people. You know the first trimester is…" She swallowed, unable to dwell any more on that horrific possibility. Instead, she switched tactics. "David and I don't want anything upstaging Lilah and Tanner's wedding."

"Oh. I think they'd be too happy for you to mind, but you guys are being really considerate." May mimed locking her lips and throwing the invisible key over her shoulder. "You can count on my discretion, sweetie. Mindy will just have to speculate alone. I won't confirm a thing."

Rachel would prefer no one was speculating anything about her at all, but that was asking too much in a town this size. "I appreciate your keeping the secret."

"Don't mention it." May grinned. "It'll be fun knowing something no one else does. Well, besides you and David, of course. You want me to make myself scarce so you can call him?"

"Actually." Rachel's fingers tightened involuntarily, and one sharp edge of the card scraped her skin. "Do you think you could spare me for a little while?"

"Absolutely! You take any time you need."

"Great." Rachel reached for the coat she'd hung on

the brass rack by the counter. "I think maybe I should go *thank* him in person."

AS SHE'D EXPECTED, Rachel found David seated at the desk in the private office behind Waide Supply. He glanced up with a smile that bordered on cocky, sending her temper through the roof.

She didn't yell, not with Arianne and Zachariah just on the other side of the wall, but her tone was pointed. "Have you *lost* your *mind?*"

"No. Why, have you found one?"

And now he was making jokes, not taking her seriously at all. "You sent me flowers. At work!"

"Well, it seemed like the best place since it's where you are during the day."

"David!" She leaned forward, bracing her hands on the desk. "This isn't funny."

His boyish smile would have melted a weaker woman. "Not even a little? Come on, most women get mad when their husbands *don't* send flowers."

"You're not my husband anymore," she said in desperation.

His humor-filled features hardened so quickly that it made him look like a different person. "The hell I'm not."

"You know what I meant. We're not married in the typical sense."

"We could be," he coaxed. "Don't you miss me, Rach? I miss you."

His tone was as dangerously addictive as really good chocolate. "Don't."

"Why not?" He rose from his chair, bracing his own

hands on the desk and angling toward her. They were practically nose to nose.

Because she couldn't recall him claiming to miss her *before* he'd heard she was pregnant. Tears pricked her eyes. Was this how she'd thoughtlessly made him feel all those months they'd been trying, as if his primary value to her was as someone who could give her a baby?

He ran his thumb across the top of her cheek, the stroke sending shivers of sensation through her. "Don't cry."

"Don't send me flowers." She straightened. "You might as well have taken out a billboard on Main Street telling everyone I'm pregnant."

"You're overreacting. It was just a basic floral arrangement. It's not like I sent one that came in a ceramic bassinet."

"No, but May and Mindy Nelson have both figured it out."

"Oh." He grimaced. "I like both of them, but if they know, the news will have spread all the way to Atlanta by morning. We should go ahead and tell my fam—"

"No! No, I'm not ready for that." She remembered the pitying glances and unsolicited platitudes from before. If, God forbid, anything should go wrong with this pregnancy, the fewer people who knew, the better.

"We shouldn't tell anyone. Not yet. Can we just get through this wedding first? Then we'll figure out the appropriate way to handle it."

He blinked. "That's uncannily like what I said to you when…"

When she'd told him she thought she should leave. He'd looked startled, then relieved, then almost coolly calculating as he'd explained why they shouldn't tell anyone yet. She hadn't thought that far ahead, merely trying to survive the moment.

She squared her shoulders, redirecting the conversation. "I know they have reputations as friendly gossips, but I don't think May or Mindy will say anything yet. At least, not anything they can back up with fact. May promised to drop the subject. I'm sure something will happen in the next day or so that's more interesting than seeing me in the pregnancy-test aisle. Without anything further to fan the flames, Mindy will probably let it go."

"You mean without incidents like me sending you ill-advised flowers?" His smile was rueful.

She softened. "They *were* beautiful."

"So are you."

"You can't say things like that!"

"We're alone. There's no May or Mindy or—"

"Rachel, are you still back here?" A blond head poked inside the doorway.

David growled. "Arianne!"

His sister hesitated. "I saw Rachel come in, but was helping a customer. I just thought I'd see if she was still around and wanted to grab an early lunch with me."

"We're kind of in the middle of something," David said.

"Not really," Rachel countered, seeing the perfect opportunity to escape. "I mean, we were, but we've finished our conversation. Ari, I'd love something to eat—I'm starving."

"Great. I'll get my purse."

Rachel made the mistake of glancing back toward

David, who mouthed, *Coward.* But then his reproving expression was replaced with a mischievous gleam that made her palms clammy and her mouth go dry.

"Hey, Ari, how about I join you?" he called. "Lunch with two of my favorite gals. I'll treat. You don't mind, do you?"

His sister grinned. "Like I'm gonna turn down free food? My mama didn't raise any fools."

David turned to Rachel and winked. "No, she sure didn't."

"You're back," May drawled, glancing up from the inventory-order forms on the counter. She smiled. "That must have been one of the longest thank-yous on record."

"Sorry. I stopped for lunch on the return trip. I can stay late to make up the time."

May waved a hand. "Not necessary. You see how swamped we are in here." Last month, they'd been busy with clients who wanted personalized Christmas cards and other holiday items, but most people who were going to purchase those had done so already.

"All right. I'll just go check the store e-mail." As Rachel sat at the computer, she could hardly concentrate enough to type in the password. Her thoughts kept drifting back to David.

He'd been utterly charming at lunch, darn him. He'd made Arianne laugh, and Rachel had reluctantly done the same. She could hardly sit through the meal glaring without letting her sister-in-law know there was a problem.

Their recent troubles had overshadowed the memories of their whirlwind courtship, how much she'd enjoyed merely being around him, how she'd smiled all the time. Lately she'd felt isolated, first by the medical side effects but most excruciatingly by losing her baby, and had been too caught up in her own suffering to notice how rare David's smiles were growing. He put on a better public face than she did, but his family hadn't been fooled. Arianne had actually commented today while they waited for the check that it had been a while since she'd seen her big brother in such a good mood.

Guilt tugged at Rachel, knowing how confused Ari would be by the forthcoming news of their separation. Of course, before she could worry about how David's family took the news, she had to make sure David himself acknowledged their separation. The flowers and his presence at lunch today made it clear that he wanted her to give it another try for their child's sake. Too much responsibility for an unborn baby. When the problems between them sharpened enough to cause discord further down the road, would one of them resent their kid for being the reason they were still together? She liked to believe that neither she nor David would ever be that petty, but she was routinely shocked by the way parents going through divorces could inadvertently hurt their children.

"Hey, I think I'm gonna go grab some lunch myself," May said. When Rachel looked up and nodded in acknowledgment, the older woman winked. "But I promise not to bring back any fish."

A few minutes later, the door opened and Belle Fulton, the executive secretary on the chamber of commerce board, bustled inside with a smile. Belle favored seriously bright shades of lipstick, so her grins were generally visible from a distance. "Happy holidays!"

Rachel grinned back. "Happy holidays to you. What can we do for you today?"

"Brochures. We're trying to attract holiday shoppers to town, increase revenue for our members."

"But—" Rachel bit her lip, realizing that her unsolicited comment was not entirely diplomatic.

Belle, however, cocked her head to the side, waiting. "Yes?"

"Nothing. I just… Are you intending to use these brochures this year? It seems like they could have done even more to attract tourist dollars if we'd printed them sooner. Not that it's any of my business," she added hastily.

Belle sighed. "No, you're right. It just takes us a while to come to any decisions and then act on them. Volunteers make up half the chamber's board, so this is on top of their normal jobs, plus we have a few very opinionated people. Then there was deciding how much it was worth to spend when we're trying to make money. The first photographer—I shouldn't even be telling you this—did such a lousy job that we had Gina Oster go back and do them over. Sweet of her, but she's hardly a pro herself. We don't have the budget for one."

Later, as Rachel put together the files to print the brochures, she couldn't help studying the pictures with a critical eye. The slogan wasn't half-bad—Nothing Says Christmas Like Mistletoe—but the pictures were far too commercial. Potential tourists and holiday shoppers didn't need to see images of the First Bank on Main Street, even if the bank *had* donated money for the project. No, what the brochure needed were homey photos of Kerrigan Farms and their rows of evergreen trees for sale. The mistletoe hanging in the white gazebo in the town square. Those were the scenes that would draw people; then once they were here, spending money would be a natural progression.

Rachel thought back to last week, when she'd half hoped for a computer error just so she had something to distract her from her personal life. No one at the chamber had asked for her input. Was she merely butting in out of self-preservation?

Maybe, she admitted, as she began typing some notes for Belle and the other directors. But needing the distraction didn't preclude also having some darn good ideas. Busy brainstorming, she barely noticed how much time had passed until May walked back in the door. With a start, Rachel sat back in her chair. When was the last time she'd been so engrossed in something, so confident in her abilities to help a client?

Okay, not a *client,* exactly. She glanced at some of what she'd written, considered the pictures she could take to bring the ideas to life. *At least, not yet.*

Chapter Eight

"All right." Rachel felt surprisingly unself-conscious about talking to her belly through the thin cotton of her pink T-shirt. "You've made your point."

Today, she and David were supposed to meet at the OB's office and find out for sure if she was pregnant. But the baby had chosen now to make its presence known beyond a shadow of a doubt. While Rachel had experienced increasing twinges of nausea in the past few weeks, this was the first time she'd truly succumbed to full-on morning sickness. The back door to the house was still open—she'd been letting the dogs out in the yard when she'd had to make a sudden run for it.

Hadn't she read somewhere that an expectant mother tossing her cookies was a sign of a healthy, growing baby?

She got to her feet slowly in case the room had any plans of spinning again, then she went into the kitchen, planning to call the dogs inside and consider breakfast options. The pregnancy books she'd bought the first time were buried in a closet back at her and David's house, but she remembered reading that, while it seemed counterintuitive, food would help *ease* the nausea. As she reached the back door, she heard the barking. She peeked her head out and saw the dogs with their noses pressed to the wooden planks of the fence. On the sidewalk beyond, David's posture was sheepish. The hounds raised enough of a ruckus to wake the entire neighborhood.

When he saw her, he called, "I was just out jogging."

"Of course." She whistled, causing the dogs to glance her way. None of them actually came toward her, however. The two older ones were at least quiet now, but Hildie kept yipping her excitement. Rachel took another step outside, wincing at the cold of the ground through her fuzzy socks. "I don't think they're going to leave their post until you pass by."

David didn't seem in any hurry. "Well, I guess I'll see you at Dr. McDermott's office…unless you want to ride together?"

It was a seemingly innocuous suggestion, yet she was left with the distinct impression he hadn't heard anything she'd tried to tell him in his office yesterday. "David—"

"You know, with gas prices being what they are," he added, "and carpooling being the more environmentally friendly option."

Exasperating man. "Sic him, Hildie."

"Honestly, Rach, what are you worried about? The few minutes alone in the car can't possibly be as intimate as the visit itself. I mean, we're going to find out for sure whether or not we've created a new life, hopefully get to see the first sonogr—"

"Shh! It's bad enough that the dogs probably woke up everyone in the subdivision. We shouldn't be out here discussing private matters."

"You're absolutely right," he said smoothly. "I'll come inside."

He went from leaning against the fence to sprinting before she had time to protest. She'd say this for him—he could move.

But paying him compliments was the furthest thing from her mind when she opened the front door. "I don't want to ride with you."

Peering at her beneath the foyer chandelier, he frowned. "Up close, you don't look... I mean... Rough morning?"

"I guess there's really no debonair way to tell a girl she's green and disheveled."

"You're sick to your stomach, aren't you? I'm an ass. You shouldn't have been standing out in the cold talking to me—you should be off your feet. Why don't you go relax, and I'll make some coffee? No, caffeine's bad for the baby. I'll pour juice and—"

"You'll go away," Rachel said firmly. "I appreciate the sentiment, sort of, but I don't need help."

"Why are you being so stubborn?"

"Why are *you?* David, I don't want you to take care of me."

He surprised her by putting a hand across her abdomen. "It's my baby, too, Rach. Let me be part of this. Don't shut me out again."

She flinched at his soft words. "I would never try to push you away where the baby's involved."

"There was a time I wouldn't have believed you would push me away, period." He let his hand drop away.

He blames me. Worse, on some level, so did she. "It's not—it's not like I set out to create distance between us. But there were times when it was hard to be around you." Like the day the doctor had called with the results from the routine test confirming that David was not the infertile one.

Of course he wasn't. Robustly healthy, he didn't even have the decency to come down with the occasional flu so that she could commiserate with other wives about what a lousy patient he was. Hell, if he ever did get sick, he'd probably be perfectly gracious about it. A tangle of long-suppressed emotion bubbled to the surface—resentment for her do-no-wrong husband and self-loathing that she hadn't been able to love him more unconditionally, that she'd ever allowed resentment to take root.

"You know, it wasn't exactly me *pushing* you, it was more pulling away. Retreating like a turtle. For my own defense."

"Defense? I never would have hurt you!"

Not on purpose, but it was amazing the accidents that could take place in close quarters. "You don't think it hurt when you pushed me to put my miscarriage behind us like it never even happened?" She cupped her hands over her belly, as if the protective gesture could somehow keep such a thing from happening again.

"I was encouraging you to look forward, to consider other possibilities. You were in such a dark place," he reminded her, frustration thick in his voice.

"I was." Tears spilled down her cheeks. "And I felt very alone there."

"I was trying my damnedest, Rach. What the hell more did you want from me?"

She struggled to find the right words, her own emotions and his growing impatience making an already difficult task nearly impossible. "Maybe what I needed was less from you."

He shoved a hand through his hair. "That doesn't even make sense."

"Well, you know me. Overwrought, crazy Rachel."

A muscle in his jaw twitched. "I can't talk to you when you're like this."

"Finally." She choked on a sob, wanting him gone so she could fall apart without losing the remains of her dignity. "Something we agree on."

"I DON'T GET men," Arianne said, leaning against the doorjamb.

"Then we're even." David kept his gaze on the spreadsheet in front of him. He needed to go in a few minutes, and he hated leaving things unfinished. "Because I don't get women." His curt tone would have warned away most would-be conversationalists.

His little sister, however, was impervious.

She sauntered inside the office and dropped into a chair. "Seriously, I'm baffled. Yesterday you were in a *great* mood. Today you're biting off heads left and right."

"You should go while yours is still attached," he said mildly.

"What's going on, Dave?" In contrast to her earlier

tone, she no longer sounded like an adolescent sibling needling him. She sounded like a bona fide grown-up who was concerned—and more astute than people might think.

He met her gaze, wanting to tell her everything was fine but unable to lie to her outright. "Nothing that we need to discuss right now. Shouldn't you be working?"

She waved a hand. "I doubt the owner will fire me over a few minutes back here. That's the beauty of nepotism."

David snorted. "Dad has never shown his kids favoritism. If anything, he's tougher on us than he's been on some of the part-time help over the years. You work darn hard."

"I know." She dimpled at him. "But I like hearing you say it. Now, are you going to tell me what's wrong, or do I have to pull Mom aside and tell her I'm dreadfully worried about you?"

"Brat." They both knew that Susan could be obstinately determined when it came to prying information from one of her kids. She'd already expressed some concern for him, and if Arianne added that he was acting strangely, his mother might not be content to leave well enough alone. He made a show of checking his watch. "If you're done with your attempted extortion, I'm supposed to meet Rachel somewhere."

"'Somewhere'?" Arianne echoed.

"It involves your Christmas present. I can't say more. It would ruin the surprise."

"You're so full of it. But at least Rach never has to worry about her husband keeping something from her. You're a lousy liar."

"I wouldn't lie to Rachel."

"I was joking. You know that, right?"

"Yeah, sure." It was just that he didn't find much about his marriage funny these days. He stood. "If I don't get out of here, I risk being late."

"Yeah, that gridlocked downtown Mistletoe traffic can be a real delay." She sighed. "Fine, don't tell me what's wrong. Go wherever it is that you're also not telling me. I'm only a blood relation, no one important."

He made it all the way to the door before he turned back to press a kiss on top of Arianne's head.

She blinked up at him. "What the heck was that?"

"I love you. You're a pain in the ass, but it's sweet that you worry about me."

"Oh God. You're not dying or something, are you?"

His laugh was rusty. "Of course not."

"All right." She raised up on her tiptoes to hug him. "Dave? Whatever is wrong, you should talk to somebody about it. If not me or Mom, then maybe Tanner. Or better yet, your wife."

He'd tried to talk to his wife—and the disastrous results were why he'd been snapping at people all day.

THE PALE BLUE chairs in the OB's waiting room were locked together bench-style, in rows of three, but Rachel and David managed to sit so rigidly that there was no chance of their bodies brushing. The silence reverberating in Rachel's skull was giving her a hell of a headache. Yet despite all of that, she was perversely relieved by David's presence.

She no longer harbored a molecule of doubt that she was pregnant, still, until she actually heard Dr. McDermott say everything was progressing just right, Rachel would remain a nervous wreck. Thank God she didn't have to await the doctor's diagnosis alone. *So much for standing on your own two feet.*

While she'd strongly wanted to throw something at her husband that morning, he'd been absolutely right on one point. *It's my baby, too, Rach. Let me be part of this.* The memory was a raw wound, substantiating what she'd known but apparently hadn't accepted: the reason she was suddenly getting the full-court press was because he didn't want to lose his place in their child's life.

Could she blame him, though? After all, he was the father.

"Rachel Waide?"

Her heart thumped against her chest. "That's me." And always would be. While she'd had her maiden name for far more years than her married surname, she didn't think she'd ever truly be comfortable as Rachel Nietermyer again. She certainly didn't want a different last name than her own child.

David had risen and was reaching automatically for her hand to help her out of the chair. She didn't pull away on purpose, it was a skittish reflex, like flinching from something coming at you in your peripheral vision. David narrowed his eyes and swiftly looked away. She wished she could take back the moment. A strangled laugh caught in her throat—if she had the power to go back in time and change even small reactions, maybe they never would have reached this point.

They followed the nurse, who handed Rachel a clear specimen cup with her name written on it. After that was taken care of, the same nurse indicated the scale. Oh, joy, just what everyone wanted—to be weighed in front of an audience. She defiantly kicked off her shoes and stepped onto the platform. Ironically, her weight was lower than she'd anticipated. Her blood pressure, however, was much higher than normal. The nurse made a concerned tutting noise as she wrote the numbers on the chart.

"I'm, uh, a little more tense today than usual," Rachel told the woman.

"Understandable. But it's best for you *and* the baby if you relax."

There were a few other minor tests to complete and medical questions to answer, although the vast majority of Rachel's history was already well-documented in her patient file. Finally, she and David were shown into a larger-than-normal exam room where an ultrasound machine sat next to the table.

"Dr. McDermott will be with you in just a few minutes. She'll most likely want to do a vaginal ultrasound."

This would be to confirm fetal age and assess viability, Rachel knew, making sure the fetus was implanted right where it should be. Her nerves started to tie themselves into knots that would impress even the most seasoned sailors.

The nurse gave them a reassuring smile. "If we're right about your being nine weeks pregnant, you'll even be able to see the heartbeat today."

Next to her, David swallowed. What was he thinking? His gorgeous face was alarmingly unreadable.

This time last year, although they were obviously having problems, Rachel would never have guessed there would come a day when he felt like a stranger to her. She had no clue whether he was remembering previous doctor's visits, if he rued the unorthodox timing of this pregnancy, if he hoped for a son or daughter… Suddenly he turned, his gaze arresting hers. Whatever he was thinking, the emotion behind it was potent.

"I'll just leave the two of you alone," the nurse said. "Mrs. Waide, you'll need to get completely undressed and put on the gown."

Gown? Fancy term for a large piece of paper with two holes on the sides and a strip meant to tie in the back. When the nurse shut the door behind her, Rachel gulped.

David wasn't meeting her gaze now. "I guess I should go wait in the hall."

Considering that she was standing there pregnant with his child, that seemed a lot like closing the barn door after the horse already got loose. "You could turn around. Promise not to look?"

"You'd trust me?" He turned toward the wall and a pink poster about new Pap smear methods.

"Trust was never the issue between us," she said. Whatever else his faults—or annoying lack thereof—it wasn't as if she'd worried David would betray her.

"I don't know," he said after a moment. "There's more than one kind of trust. What you said today about needing to protect yourself from getting hurt…"

There was a raw pain in his voice she hadn't expected, and she paused in the act of unfastening her bra. He was keeping his word, not watching her, which presented an unusual opportunity to look her fill. He wasn't basketball-player tall, but he was a nice height for her, strong and solid. His posture had always been correct; no one needed to remind him to stand up straight. Even so, there was a slight rounding to his broad shoulders, the tiniest sign of dejection. Or defeat.

"David, I wasn't trying to hurt you with what I said this morning." She folded her bra inside her discarded shirt, then reached for the waistband of her pants. This was a surreal conversation to be having while she stripped.

His laugh held no traces of humor. "See? We really don't trust each other. You weren't trying to hurt me, I wasn't trying to hurt you. So why, instead of giving the other person the benefit of the doubt, do we jump to the worst conclusions?"

Because love made people vulnerable.

She couldn't voice the thought without admitting that she still loved him, not in the bright, think-about-you-all-the-time way she had when she'd first met him. This was more bittersweet and weather-beaten. They'd shared so much, both good and bad. They'd grown apart like vines reaching for separate suns instead of becoming stronger together, but the memories they'd created would never fade completely. *Especially since we created something a lot more tangible than a memory.* She splayed her fingers over her navel.

"You almost done?" he asked, shifting his weight restlessly.

She grabbed for the paper wrapper. "Just about."

"I can't believe I'm alone in a room with you, you're finally naked, and *I'm* stuck reading about innovations in cervical health."

An errant giggle escaped her. "Sorry."

"Really?" His shoulders straightened. "Because there are ways you could make it up to me."

"Not that sorry."

"Yeah, that's what I figured."

There were two quick knocks on the door outside before Lydia McDermott stuck her head inside. "Everyone decent?"

"We're ready." Rachel scooted onto the table as the beaming doctor entered the room.

"So it looks like congrats are in order! The two of you must be thrilled," Dr. McDermott said.

Rachel cleared her throat. "We're…a lot of things. Surprised, for one. After all those months of trying, and then after we'd pretty much concluded we were giving up, *bam*."

The doctor nodded. "You'd be surprised how it happens that way for many people. Couples who find out they're pregnant halfway through adoption proceedings, or couples who have just adopted a baby and then find out another one is coming. The mind and body connection is a funny thing. It's as if for some couples, once they accept that it's not going to happen—as you said—bam, it does."

"The universe has a sick sense of humor. Not that I'm complaining," Rachel added hastily, not wanting to test fate. David came to stand beside her.

Dr. McDermott was a tall, aristocratic-looking woman who delivered dozens of babies each year. Though her sleek bob had gone almost entirely gray, her blue eyes twinkled and her attractive face was mostly unlined. She looked wise and capable.

Rachel knew with sudden certainty she didn't want

anyone but Lydia delivering this baby. *I'm staying in Mistletoe.* Which meant she had to decide on some long-term plans, the sooner, the better. She couldn't stay at Winnie's until the baby came this summer.

The doctor wore reading glasses on a slim chain around her neck and lifted them to better study the nurse's notes. "How are you feeling? Any major side effects you want to discuss or ask about?"

"Well, the morning sickness has kicked in. That was fun," Rachel said wryly. "And I was cramping a few days ago. Before the home pregnancy test. At the time, I figured it was just my stalled period about to start."

"We'll check everything out, of course, but lots of women experience abdominal discomfort from ligaments stretching. Things are moving around and changing, so there will be some minor pains. Don't let them panic you. Any headaches, dizziness or breast tenderness?"

"Yes, on all three counts." Thinking about how sensitive her breasts had become—it practically hurt to roll over in her sleep—Rachel felt herself blush. They'd always been sensitive, which, in happier times, David had used to orgasmic effect.

"All right." Dr. McDermott walked to the counter and set down the manila folder. "Why don't you lie back, and we'll take a look."

Rachel's heart fluttered rapidly. As she reclined, she reached out without thinking. David reacted immediately, clasping her hand and giving it a brief reassuring squeeze. She couldn't look at him—it would make the moment too unbearably intimate—but she was grateful for the contact.

If she stopped to think about what was going on, the ultrasound would have been a bit embarrassing, but she was far too mesmerized by the colors and blobs on the small screen Dr. McDermott turned toward her.

"There. See that? There's your little one, right where he should be." A tiny shape, curved but indistinct, a dark winking at the center.

Tears blurred Rachel's vision. That was her baby, that was the heartbeat.

David sounded choked up as well when he asked, "It was just a figure of speech, right? The 'he'? I mean you can't tell…"

Dr. McDermott chuckled. "No, it'll be a long time before I can advise you whether to buy pink paint or blue, but the months will go fast. You're already well on your way to the second trimester! As anxious as the two of you have been, I'm surprised you didn't take the home test sooner."

How to explain that she'd been so preoccupied with her marriage falling apart that the first missed period had gone unnoticed? "Well, I was afraid to get my hopes up too soon."

Lydia nodded, pressing some buttons on her machine. "Give it a few minutes, and you'll have your first baby picture for the scrapbook. Everything looks great."

Once the exam was over, they talked some more about what to expect and when Rachel should come back in for the next visit.

"That's everything for now," the doctor concluded. "I'll step out and let you get dressed, give you a chance to think of any more questions. And a moment to celebrate your good news privately." She smiled at both of them, then left.

Neither of them moved. David looked as poleaxed as Rachel felt.

He glanced at the grainy photo Dr. McDermott had handed him. "We did that."

She grinned over his shoulder. "Yeah."

"Wow."

"Yeah." The enormity of the situation settled over her; she and David had created *life*. There was a new little person growing inside her. Even though she'd known it on an abstract level, seeing the visual proof was profound.

"You all right?" he asked.

"I'll be better once we hit the second trimester mark," she admitted.

"'We'? Meaning you and the baby?"

"All of us." She stopped, started again. "I'm still going to see my family in a few weeks, but just temporarily. Whatever else happens, I won't leave Mistletoe until the baby's born."

He closed his eyes for a moment. "And after?"

"I…I'm still working on that."

Not an answer he liked, but all she could give him was the truth. Whatever he might be thinking, he didn't argue. Instead, he selected another wall to face—this time with a view of a smaller brochure printed on bright pink paper. Rachel slid her feet down over the side of the exam table. In the quiet of the room, the sounds of paper rasping against her skin and the slide of fabric seemed exaggerated. Within minutes, she was completely dressed and slipping on her shoes.

"All done," she said.

"Rach?" He turned his head, his blue-green eyes burning like turquoise flame. "If I had asked you not to go, if I had asked you to see a marriage therapist with me first, to try working this all out…would you have agreed to give us another shot?"

Her chest constricted so tightly she couldn't breathe. "I think I would have," she said after a long moment's thought. "If you'd asked *before* you knew about the baby, I would have."

Chapter Nine

After the doctor's appointment, David's mind was too cluttered for him to go back to work. If he tried crunching numbers in this mental state, the store would probably never recover from all the data errors. *I could single-handedly destroy generations' worth of work in an afternoon.* Something approximating a smile tugged at the corners of his lips. The despairing thought was the kind of exaggerated, self-deprecating statement he used to fuss at Rachel for making.

Lord, he missed her. If she didn't move back into the house, he'd eventually put it up for sale. Without her there, it just felt...wrong. He was grateful beyond words that she wasn't going anywhere at least until summer, but the possibility of losing her after that, of losing his child, was too painful to entertain.

Once home, he wandered through the rooms like a ghost, seeing the things they'd picked out together, trying to recall which pieces had been wedding presents. In their room, he opened the dresser drawer where she stored her summer clothes, skimming his hand over the fabrics, thinking about how pretty she'd always looked in the pale green tank top. With ninety percent of her belongings still here, it seemed as if she was just out at the store and would be home any minute, where she belonged.

At the knock on the door, he started. Was it Rach? Maybe there was something she needed to make her more comfortable over at Winnie's.... He dashed through the house at twice the speed he'd moved earlier.

Tanner waved at him through the beveled glass in the front door.

David sighed. "Hey. Come on in."

"I called you at the store, but Arianne said you went home early today."

"Had some errands to run," David said vaguely. "Want something to drink?"

"Sure. I'll take a cold beer if you've got one."

David retrieved two bottles from the refrigerator. "So, did Ari send you over here?"

Tanner looked surprised by the question. "She told me you were probably here, but I'm not here at her bidding or anything. I swung by on my way home from a client's to beg a favor."

"Beg away." Maybe David should try the same approach. Should he grovel to Rachel? His pride balked at the idea, but that didn't matter nearly as much as the prospect of growing old without her. Even now, with the two of them under different roofs, he couldn't truly imagine life without her.

"Lilah wants to take a day trip this weekend, go somewhere more exotic than Mistletoe for all her Christmas shopping." Tanner pulled a face, making it clear marathon shopping wasn't his idea of a good time. "Misery loves company, right?"

David sipped his beer. "You want me to come shopping with the two of you?"

"Well, you and Rachel. We thought the four of us could head toward Atlanta, eat dinner someplace together before coming back. All of our single friends are getting a little sick of the constant wedding chatter. I'll be the first to admit, we're nauseating. We thought it would be fun to spend time with another couple who won't hold it against us. What do you say, got plans for the weekend?"

David brightened. An entire day in Rachel's company? "Sounds great."

"You heard the part about the all-day shopping, right? No doubt there will be sales and shoes involved."

"There are worse things in the world, little brother." David took a deep breath, then pushed away the negative emotions. Winners used positive thinking, no matter what odds they faced. "I just have to check with Rachel. Call you tomorrow?"

"Sure. You're not kicking me out already, are you? I haven't finished the beer."

"No, you can stick around. If you want, I could order us a pizza."

"Sorry, dude. I have a preexisting offer from someone a lot prettier. Then again…" Tanner studied him. "If you need me to stay, I can call Lilah and cancel."

"No, of course not. I was just making the offer to be polite."

Tanner leaned against the counter. "Why did you

think Arianne sent me over here? Did you two fight or something?"

"Or something."

"I'm a little surprised you're not doing the pizza thing with Rachel." He glanced around as if he, too, could feel her absence despite all appearances being normal. "I know she's sleeping at Winnie's because someone has to stay with the dogs, but she gets dinner breaks, right?"

"Of course. In fact, I'll call her as soon as you leave. I just thought maybe a night of male bonding before you take your vows…"

Tanner laughed. "I'm sure we'll have plenty of time for that even after. There's a limit to what my getting married is going to change."

That's what you think.

David could look back and see lots of big and small ways that Rachel had changed over the years and ways that their relationship had altered—would that he'd been paying more attention at the time. Hindsight was painfully clear. What was harder to see, even now, was how *he'd* changed. Rachel had loved him so much once. Had he not been what she expected somehow? He wasn't objective enough to evaluate himself as a husband.

Granted, he probably could have handled Rachel's losing the baby better, but he'd been mourning, too. As much as she'd wanted that child, he doubted he could have said or done anything to make it better. Knowing that had doubled his own grief. He knew that the specter of what had happened before loomed over her now, and he hated like hell that she was alone in the house with three dogs, worrying, when he was two streets over and unable to help. *Three dogs.* Rembrandt and Bristol weren't small. All three of them were excitable—what if one of them forgot his manners and jumped up on Rachel?

"If you're about finished," David said, "I think I *am* going to kick you out."

"Nothing like brotherly love. All right, I'll get out of your hair. Let me know what Rachel says about holiday shopping this weekend? Just think, Christmas is right around the corner, and then the wedding." Tanner's expression was luminous enough to power the entire town.

David assessed the younger man, the rebel who'd once seemed as though he might never mature past his angry restlessness. "Look at you, all grown up and about to marry a wonderful woman. I'm proud of you."

"Thanks." Tanner's gaze landed on an old souvenir photo-magnet of Rachel and David on the refrigerator. "You didn't do so badly for yourself, either."

They each finished their beer, then Tanner set his bottle on the counter. "I'm leaving before this deteriorates into something truly scary, like hugging."

David shuddered. "That would be bad."

After Tanner left, David rifled through the junk drawer in the kitchen, looking for the delivery number for that pizzeria Rachel liked.

The girl who answered confirmed his name and asked, "Is this 820 Pine?"

"Yes, but I'd actually like to get this delivered to another address...."

"I HAVE A proposition," he blurted as soon as she opened the door.

Rachel looked heavenward. "This can't be good."

"You're such a glass-half-empty person."

"It's called being a realist." Her voice was dry but amusement danced in her eyes. "It helps offset people like you who occasionally suffer delusions of grandeur."

"Well, see there, we balance each other out," he said as he came inside.

He was glad to see that her cheeks had some nice color to them. She looked girlishly comfortable in a pair of pink drawstring pants and a T-shirt, far healthier than she had when he'd seen her right after her bout of morning sickness. He'd had so much to think about today that their daybreak encounter seemed like eons ago. *Let's try this again.* This time, without his good intentions devolving into an argument.

Rachel was waiting expectantly, her arms folded across her chest. Watching her, he couldn't help recalling the doctor's question about whether her breasts were sensitive…and Rachel's near-blush when she'd answered. And how long it had been since he'd really touched her. Their spontaneous kiss on Saturday had only whetted his appetite for more.

He should probably stop thinking about that. He should also stop staring at the round, full swell of her breasts beneath the lightweight cotton.

"David? You had something you wanted to talk to me about?"

"Move back home."

"What? But—"

"Not with me," he clarified. "I'll stay here."

She walked into the living room, and he followed. He would have liked to sit with her on the couch, but that would put him in maddening proximity to those wonderful curves. He chose a striped wing chair instead.

"It's quiet," he noted.

"The dogs are out back." She tucked her feet up under her. "Either they didn't hear you approach, or they've just gotten used to you."

"I think they like me," he said. "Which works out nicely since I'm proposing you let me take care of them."

She shook her head, her smile rueful. "You're just not happy without others to look after, are you? It seems irresponsible to dump them on you. I made a promise to Winnie."

"That her animals would be in good hands, and they will be. You'd be more comfortable at home, wouldn't you? Sleeping in your own bed." He lightened his tone. "Or at least hurling in the privacy of your own bathroom."

"Ew."

"No offense to Winnie, but her mutts aren't the most disciplined in the world. Just look at last week when you tried to walk them and Hildie got away." As soon as he said it, he knew he'd made a tactical misstep. Rachel was scowling. "Of course, that could have happened to anyone."

"Probably not to you," she grumbled.

"Never mind. What happened the other morning wasn't really my point, I was just grasping for an example. What about the cat? Isn't there something about pregnant women not being around litter boxes? And what if one of those dogs jumped up on you? Rach." He glanced at her belly, trying to imagine what it would look like as it expanded with their child, wishing he could kiss her right above her belly button. "According to Dr. McDermott, everything looks great with the pregnancy. Why take any unnecessary chances, even small ones?"

Rachel hesitated, obviously pondering the points he'd made. Then she laughed. "Does it ever get exhausting, being right all the time? Still…I feel weird about swapping places without Winnie's permission."

"I'll be a model pet-care provider," he swore.

"There are five of them, counting the rabbit. The instructions were pretty lengthy."

He smiled, sensing victory. "We can talk about it over pizza. Which should be here in about five more minutes."

"David!" She laughed as she said it, a good sign.

"I've missed your laugh," he told her, knowing he was probably pushing his luck but unable to stop himself. "I've missed seeing you happy."

"I've missed *being* happy."

He sat forward. "And you think you will be without me?"

"I don't know. I know I wasn't happy with who I became with you. That's not blame," she added quickly. "Not anymore. I was going through a lot and somehow ended up feeling like a second-class citizen. And logical or not, the resentment I was stifling turned me into someone petulant. Someone I don't recognize and don't want to become."

"I want to apologize," he said slowly, determined not to repeat this morning when they'd each said whatever popped into their minds and left each other with fresh scars. "But it feels disingenuous when I'm confused about what I'm supposed to be sorry for. A second-class citizen? That's…"

"What, ridiculous?"

Yes. "Everyone in Mistletoe knows how much I love you," he insisted. "I went out of my way to do things for you."

She ran a hand through her hair. "I know. And yet you just proved my point. I tried to share something difficult and personal, something I'm not proud of, and your response, no matter how polite, was to tell me why I was wrong."

"That's not what I was doing! You—" He broke off, catching himself that time. "Hmm."

She laughed, taking pity on him. "If you're serious about taking care of the animals, follow me. I'll show you where the rabbit is, and we'll see if we can convince Arpeggio to come out from under whatever bed she's chosen this time. Winnie said that the cat is still sulking about the puppy and has been fairly antisocial lately."

With the dogs outside, they were able to coax Arpeggio out from under the guest room bed. The tricolor cat hobbled out, its gaze curious but its ears twitching back with suspicion as it approached David. He waited patiently, stretching his hand out and sitting perfectly still until the cat rubbed up against his fingers. Then he began scratching her back in earnest, and the calico started purring.

"See?" David said softly. "I'm not so bad."

Rachel sat on the carpet next to him. "I can't believe

I don't know the answer to this, but did you have pets growing up?"

"A few hamsters with short life spans," he said. "Arianne had one of those beta fish. Dad's allergic to cats and Mom's allergic to dogs. They had a poodle when they were first married, but I don't really remember her. What about you?"

"My mom was dead set against pets and I never really thought much about it. But Hildie's been growing on me, despite my occasionally wanting to throttle her. Maybe I'll get a dog," Rachel mused.

Maybe I'll *get a dog.* Ouch. It should have been something they'd done together. Why had he never considered during those long, frustrated months when she had so much love to give but no baby to lavish it upon, that she might appreciate a fuzzy friend who cuddled by her side when she was blue? Instead of just telling her to cheer up or have hope, he could have surprised her with a pet rescued from the local animal shelter. He'd asked himself—and her—what more he could have done, but maybe that was a cop-out. In retrospect, there was probably more he could have tried. Had he truly worked at staying emotionally connected with his wife or had he assumed, because of their vows, that she'd always be there?

Till death do us part. A lofty goal, but had he really worked toward it the way he did other aspirations? He'd once coached four-year-olds in the community soccer program, and they were hysterical to watch. They understood the basics, that the ball was supposed to go into the goal, but some of them seemed to think those events would just unfold, as they milled around on the field, not really making the connection between what they wanted to achieve and their own part in making it happen.

Maybe Tanner would be a better husband than David had been. He'd lost Lilah once. Having to win her back helped ensure that he appreciated her worth, knew how miserable he'd been without her.

David's experience might be coming later in life, but he liked to think he was a quick study. "Hey, I talked to Tanner earlier. He wanted to ask us a favor."

"Does he need something for the wedding?"

"Actually, no, he wanted to recruit us for some Christmas shopping."

"You mean he's looking for help finding Lilah a present?"

"He wanted to know if we'd go with them out of town this weekend for a holiday shopping spree."

The doorbell gonged, startling them both.

"That'll be the pizza." David stood, reaching for the wallet in his jeans pocket. "Is it okay that I took care of dinner plans?"

"In theory, it was high-handed." She smiled up at him. "In practice, I am a pregnant woman who didn't entirely realize how hungry she was *or* how tired she was getting until about ten minutes ago. And here you are, summoning food as if by magic. So you're forgiven. This once."

He grinned over his shoulder as he walked down the stairs. "It's a start."

Chapter Ten

Rachel drove to the print shop the next morning feeling surprisingly rejuvenated. She'd dropped off to sleep as soon as David had left, and their dinner together had been…enjoyable. Almost relaxed, as if, with the strain of holding their marriage together lifted, they could just be themselves. In some ways, having the worst happen could be liberating. They'd agreed that he should take over the pet-sitting, but she'd been too tired to switch places with him last night.

Tonight she'd go home. She still had mixed feelings about that, but she'd cope. She was already dealing with separating from David, the—happy—shock of being pregnant and compiling a mental list of the decisions she'd need to start making for herself and the baby. None of it was easy, but it wasn't impossible, either.

"Morning, May," she called when she walked into work.

Her boss waved her own hello over a mug of coffee. "Miss Popularity! You've already had two phone calls this morning."

"You're kidding. Who from?"

"Both from Gina Oster, at the chamber of commerce. Belle showed her some of the recommendations you made for future Christmas brochures, and they want to talk to you about some projects for the spring." May grinned. "You're not thinking of leaving me for greener pastures, are you?"

"Don't worry. I doubt a chamber the size of ours can afford much green," Rachel said realistically. "But I can talk to them about some cheap independent contracting on the side." She found herself really eager to return Gina's call. While Rachel didn't see the chamber as being a career move for her, it was exciting to think about ways she could use her talents to give back to the town. Mistletoe had given her so much.

"Well, Gina's in meetings until this afternoon. That's why she was trying to reach you so early, but if you can help them get organized, I think it's a wonderful idea. You've been such an asset to me."

Rachel was touched by the warm sincerity in the woman's voice. "Thank you."

She'd spent so much time lately feeling under-utilized in her current career that she'd lost sight of how lucky she was. She worked for a nice person she genuinely liked, she didn't have to wear panty hose and she wasn't bogged down in meetings and corporate bureaucracy. And on particularly busy days, she helped balance a workload no person could manage alone.

It shaped up to be one of those days. They printed a last-minute batch of flyers for the Winter Wonderland dance that would go up all over town, farmed out a rush order for some customized baseball caps, then printed and bound a series of booklets for an upcoming business retreat. She thought about the hiking vacation she'd taken here, the lodge that was just outside town and more rustic than the popular Mistletoe Inn. The chamber of commerce should do more to play up their appeal as a place to "come get away from it all…without having to go too far" for businessmen and even vacationing tourists.

Mistletoe, a great place to bring the family. A great place to raise a family.

"Well, you're in a good mood."

She jumped about a foot, then turned to see David. Nonemployees weren't allowed behind the counter where all the equipment was kept, but May would have made an exception to wave him back. "I thought I was alone. Just me and the forty booklets I promised to assemble by lunch."

David shoved his hands in his pockets. "Didn't mean to startle you. In fact, I would have been happy just to stand here and watch."

"Watch me collate booklets? Make sure you stick around for the exciting encore of watching paint dry in the storeroom."

He laughed. "Don't sell yourself short. You're way more interesting than paint."

"Thanks, I think."

"You had a graceful rhythm going, complete with intermittent musical accompaniment. What were you whistling?" he asked.

"I was whistling? I was just…thinking about family."

His gaze went instantly to her tummy then came back up to meet hers. "Excited about junior?"

"Giddy," she agreed. "But not just about that. I was sort of counting my blessings."

It wasn't until he looked away that she saw how hurtful her words might be. Was it unseemly to seem so cheerfully content in front of the husband you'd recently left? She was content, though. For the first time in a long time, she was starting to believe that she'd be all right no matter what. That she could survive disappointments and missteps and pick herself up afterward. It was an empowering realization.

"Well," he said quickly. "I just came by to get Winnie's key."

"Right." Her duffel bags were packed and in the trunk of her car. She'd still feel better if she could talk with Winnie about it first, but shore-to-ship communications were spotty at best. She went to her purse and grabbed the bone-shaped key ring. "Here you go. If the dogs give you any trouble or you can't find Arpeggio—"

With a wicked grin, David cut her off. "I've got it all under control. If I do have any problems, I know where to find you."

She bit the inside of her lip to keep from laughing at the role reversal. "Of course you're completely competent. I was just trying to be helpful."

"Believe me, I know the feeling." He leaned forward, surprising her with a quick kiss on her cheek. "Pick you up Saturday?" It really didn't make sense for them to drive separately to Lilah's duplex just to pile into Tanner's car once they arrived.

Rachel nodded. "I'm looking forward to it." She

really was, not only to the fun of shopping and laughing with Lilah, but to being in David's company again soon.

Which meant either she and David were the most mature, well-adjusted couple ever to split or that her romantic feelings for her husband hadn't cooled nearly as much as she'd let herself believe.

WALKING into the house was like taking a one-way trip to Rachel's past. She set her keys on the dented antique table in the front hall—they'd bought it for a great price at this little flea market because of scratches on the surface. David had wanted to restore it, but she liked the imperfections, thought they provided more character than a glossy veneer could. The silence echoed around her, unnatural. Had it always been so quiet here? She'd grown accustomed to the considerable background noise at Winnie's house. Here, there were no animals, only wall-to-wall memories.

She slid out of her shoes and went straight to the kitchen. Despite grappling with nausea these days, she was *starving*. Some men living on their own might have cupboards devoid of anything but basic guy staples, but the refrigerator boasted a huge selection of produce, marinated chicken breasts, organic eggs, three types of fruit juice and a nearly full gallon of milk. The freezer was also stocked with an array of choices. She made herself a three-egg omelet with mushrooms, cheese, peppers, broccoli florets and a side of whole-grain toast. Afterward, when she was pleasantly stuffed, she decided she should work on the scrapbook she and Ari planned to give Lilah and Tanner at their rehearsal dinner.

It had been Arianne's idea, although Rachel freely admitted that not only did her sister-in-law take lousy pictures—half of which included her thumb over the lens—she was no good at arranging them artfully. "You have an eye for these things," Ari had wheedled.

"In other words, you're hoping I'll do all the work," Rachel had translated with a laugh.

"In a nutshell."

With Quinn's help, the two of them had been surreptitiously gathering pictures from half the people in town. Rachel would be shocked if Lilah and Tanner hadn't caught wind of it yet. Mistletonians weren't known for their ability to keep secrets. Rachel had an assortment of childhood pictures, sweetheart photos from when the couple had first dated back in high school, individual milestone shots, such as college graduations and Lilah's first day teaching, and more recent mementos from the previous year, when they'd rekindled their romance. Even though Rachel had been happy to help with the project, she'd been procrastinating. Laying out a visual representation of another couple's romance while her own was in decline had been difficult.

Now just the opposite was happening. Sure, there was a melancholy twinge when she looked at the timeline of Lilah and Tanner's love spread out across her coffee table, but staring at their memories, she was also caught up in her own. Good ones. As she cut and glued and sorted through her collection of stamps and die-cut embellishments, she found herself unconsciously whistling again. She paused, replaying the melody in her mind to figure out what it was.

"Raindrops Keep Fallin' On My Head."

Just as she was debating turning on the radio versus the television for background noise, the phone rang.

"Hello?"

"It's me," David said. "I just wanted to let you know there's a rerun of *Lost* on TV tonight."

"Oh. Okay, thanks."

"It's a repeat, but I'm pretty sure it's that one you missed last fall."

Because she'd misprogrammed the VCR, she remembered, taping an hour's worth of some completely random channel. "That's sweet, David, but I caught that episode. Watched it online."

There was a pause. "You saw it without me?" They'd watched the show together from the very first episode, speculating during commercials, each having different theories about where the storylines were going and how to tell when Ben was lying (when his lips were moving).

"Sorry," she said, meaning it. Funny with everything that each of them could legitimately regret about their relationship how bad she suddenly felt about watching an hour of television alone. "You haven't seen it?"

"No. It's on in about ten minutes. I was planning to get the dogs settled and sit down with a sandwich for dinner."

"I'll turn it on, too," she decided. "You know how that show is. There are always clues you miss the first time around."

Once they got off the phone, she got the remote control out of the side pocket of David's recliner and found the right channel. During the second commercial break, David called to ask her if the episode was going to conclude the way he thought—it wasn't—and then laughingly argued with her when she refused to tell him how it did end.

"Just wait and see," she teased. "I kind of like you *not* having all the answers for a change."

"Gee, thanks." The casual affection in his tone belied his words. "Have you been taking brat lessons from Ari?"

"I'm hanging up on you now," she informed him. "Show's coming back on."

Half an hour later, he called back during another commercial break trying to remember where he'd seen one of the guest actors before.

"You know, that's the sort of thing you could find in about thirty seconds on the Internet," she pointed out, holding her breath. Would he tell her that the calls weren't just about the show? Perhaps he looked forward to talking to her the same way she was looking forward to seeing him again on Saturday.

"Yeah, but if I go online, I'm going to look up the episode and see how it ends. I have no willpower."

She snorted, thinking of his dedicated jogging regimen and the way he pursued goals with determination. "What a crock."

"Well." His voice went lower. "I have more self-discipline when it comes to some things than others."

She sat a little straighter on the couch. "Really?"

"Really. I keep entertaining these thoughts that I tell myself are inappropriate, but it hasn't stopped me from thinking them." He paused. "Anything like that ever happen to you?"

Only whenever she saw him. Or heard his voice. Or thought of him. "Yeah, as a matter of fact."

"Any tips on how to handle it?"

Oh, sure—the one time David asked for advice from her, she was clueless what to tell him. "You got me."

"All evidence to the contrary." He said it lightly, but there was a noticeable undercurrent.

He misses me. Whether his feelings were spawned by learning about the baby or by the fragile new peace between them or by nostalgia from the preparations for the upcoming wedding, she didn't doubt that the emotion was legitimate. It wasn't fair that they were getting along better apart than they had together. Was it because they were both so happy about the baby? It was easier to get along when things were going well, but would their renewed friendship withstand future hardships? That's where they'd stumbled before. *For better or worse.* The latter was clearly the more difficult to master.

The blaring notes of some show's theme song jolted her attention back to the television, where opening credits were rolling. She reached for the remote. "We missed the rest of *Lost.*"

He groaned. "Okay, now you *have* to tell me how it ended."

Once she'd obligingly filled him in, they said their good-nights. With the television off and David gone, the house was more hushed than ever. Unable to get back into her scrapbooking groove, she decided to get ready for bed. *And sleep where?*

The logical choice was probably the larger quality mattress in the master bedroom, but she hadn't slept there in over a month. Pondering, she flipped on the hallway light and walked to the would-be nursery where she'd spent her most recent nights in the house.

The room looked different even though nothing discernible had changed. It seemed bigger, somehow, not a place where she felt trapped anymore but a space of infinite possibilities. She thought back to her time on the phone with David, and optimism bubbled inside her. Was there a chance that, by the time they learned this baby's gender, Rachel would be living in the house with him? She imagined sitting next to him in bed, poring over magazines together, eyeing pink teddy bear motifs or sports mobiles with soccer balls and baseballs.

"I can't wait," she said aloud. Was it strange to talk to your belly? "I can't wait to meet you. We already love you so much."

Having struggled through the tough decisions— whether to take the drugs, when it was time to stop, whether they should try again—she was exhilarated by the prospect of making the *fun* decisions. The nursery theme, buying cute little outfits, adding cartoons to her movie collection and finding copies of beloved children's books. She decided not to sleep in here, whether because of superstition or because she wouldn't get any rest staring at the walls and trying to picture how different borders and stencils would look, but she took one long last look before turning off the light.

Infinite possibilities. A phrase that suddenly seemed to apply not just to this room, but her life.

"THANKS AGAIN for agreeing to this," David said, his grateful smile making him so appealing that Rachel lost her breath for a minute.

I want to kiss him. She turned toward the door under the pretext of trying the handle and making sure she'd locked it. "Don't mention it."

She hadn't done any Christmas shopping and, like everything else in her life, she had a lot of catching up to do. Plus, she truly adored Tanner and Lilah. It promised to be an enjoyable day. For all that one heard about pregnancy mood swings, in a way, she was more serene than she had been in months.

"How are you feeling this morning?" David asked as they walked down the driveway. "Everything all right with you and the little one?"

"We're great." She broke into a wide smile as a thought struck her. "Just think, if all goes well, this time next year junior will be experiencing his or her first Christmas."

David grinned with her. "And we'll get our first shot at playing Santa. I'll bet…" He trailed off, his smile fading.

"It's a year away," she said gently. "A lot could happen." She didn't want to make false promises or rush to any decisions, but she was going to keep an open mind.

Even if she and David parted ways as planned, she had every intention of making this split amicable and working out the best possible custody situation for all three of them. Still, the harsh truth was that no method of sharing birthdays and divvying up holidays could replace living together, having both parents there for every milestone. Her heart stuttered. What if she missed the first time their baby rolled over or slept through the night, what if she missed the first step? She couldn't bear the idea, but she couldn't begrudge David those moments, either.

His manner subdued, he opened her door for her.

"So, your mom came by to get the key from you?" she asked, fishing for conversation.

"Yeah. I told her we both really appreciated it."

Susan, who'd once been Winnie's Sunday-school teacher, would let the dogs out around lunch. Rachel had asked Tanner and Lilah if they could have an early dinner and return from their day of shopping in time for someone to give the pooches adequate attention this evening. David had promised to take them for a long walk if it wasn't too cold.

It was only a short drive to Lilah's. Tanner had his own apartment for the time being, but would move in with Lilah after the wedding while they waited for their house to be finished. After some weather delays and switching contractors in the middle of construction, Lilah had grumbled that the next time they had the bright idea to build their own house, she was buying stock in aspirin. Nevertheless, Rachel thought it was romantic that Lilah and Tanner had put such effort and thought into planning their future together, starting from the steel-reinforced concrete foundation and working their way up.

Lilah opened the front door before they even had a chance to knock. "Hey, guys." She hugged both of them. "Tanner just ran back to the kitchen to grab a cookie tin."

"Road-trip provisions," her husband-to-be called.

"We're not going to be on the road that long," Lilah reminded him, smiling indulgently. "Thank heavens for Tanner. This might be the first year I don't gain ten pounds from the holiday treats my students bring in."

Tanner appeared in the hallway behind her, twirling his car keys. Tucked under his other arm was a blue tin painted with snowflakes. "So, are we all set to hit the road?"

Just as David was saying yes, Rachel interrupted, "Actually, Lilah, would you mind if I use your bathroom first?"

"Be my guest."

There was nothing remarkable in Rachel's request—the first time—but she was sure Tanner and Lilah were surprised when she asked him to pull over for their *third* pit stop before they reached the shopping megaplex.

"Feeling okay?" Lilah asked as she held her hands under an automatic dryer.

Rachel rubbed her own hands together under the water. "Absolutely. Just a small bladder." With a tiny person growing on top of it.

"I was thinking, when we get there, we should split up—guys and girls?"

"Yes!"

Lilah laughed at Rachel's eager agreement. "Guess you're not done shopping for David, either, huh?"

More like she hadn't even started. They were spending Christmas Day with the Waides, opening presents together as they had for the past four years. She didn't have the first clue what to get him this year. Everything felt wrong.

"I know it's hypocritical," Lilah was saying, "my

always admonishing the kids not to procrastinate when I've put off almost all of my shopping until a week and a half before Christmas, but I've been so preoccupied with the wedding."

"Understandable." Rachel reached for the door.

"I've at least been thinking about what I want to buy, so it's not complete procrastination, right? I think Tanner did all his shopping on the Internet, but I'm old-fashioned." Lilah grinned. "I like the crowds, the fruitless hunt for a parking spot, the canned carols playing overhead."

Rachel laughed. "Yeah, nothing says happiest time of the year like lamenting that they're all sold out of the size you need while you're listening to 'Santa Claus Is Coming to Town' for the fifth time that day."

"Exactly!"

As they walked down the sidewalk toward the car, Lilah nodded toward the two men waiting within. "If we split up, maybe it'll give the guys a chance to talk."

"About?"

Lilah faltered. "Oh. Well, I don't know specifically. I should have thought before I babbled."

"Lilah, what is it?"

The redhead averted her gaze. "Tanner would probably feel self-conscious if he knew I was saying this."

"Don't worry, he won't hear it from me."

"It's just that, lately, he's had the feeling something's on David's mind." Lilah looked even more uncomfortable. "Probably nothing, stuff at the store or whatever."

"Mmm." Rachel kept her expression determinedly noncommittal.

"People who don't know him well wouldn't see it,

but Tanner can be really sensitive. He's the younger brother and was the family screwup."

Rachel waved a hand. "Nobody thinks of him that way."

"*He* does sometimes. I think it would mean a lot if, for a change, his respected older brother came to him for advice." Lilah's face went soft with affection. "Tanner would never put it this way, but I think the big lug just wants to feel needed. Like he's graduated to a point where David considers him his equal."

Rachel felt a pang of sympathy for her brother-in-law. *Buddy, I know how you feel.*

Chapter Eleven

"You buy anything else for your bride-to-be and you're gonna need a pack mule." David watched his brother shift bags to balance weight distribution.

"Mock all you want," Tanner rejoined. "Your harassment is nothing compared to hugs and kisses from a happy Lilah on Christmas morning."

David barely heard anything after *kisses*. The taste of Rachel's kiss had been taunting him all week, particularly today, as they'd sat close together in the backseat of Tanner's compact car. She glowed with an expression of sublime contentment—he didn't think he'd ever seen a more beautiful woman. More than once, he'd seen her hand go to her abdomen, a quick gesture of affection toward their unborn child. He knew she didn't realize she was doing it, but if she kept it up, May Gideon and Mindy Nelson wouldn't be the only ones to clue in to the pregnancy.

Fine with me. Whenever he thought about Rachel having his baby, he wanted to shout the news from the rooftops. Could there be a more amazing Christmas gift for his mom and dad than telling them they were going to be grandparents? He could imagine Zachariah's gruff expression of pride, his turning away because he'd never become entirely comfortable with anyone seeing emotion on his face. Susan, on the other hand, would sob unabashedly, gathering David and Rachel both in a group hug. His parents had always loved her.

They'd be devastated when she left. How was he going to explain it? His pulse thundered. *I can't let it come to that.*

"Tanner, if you did something, if you messed things up with Lilah…"

"You mean like move away with only a note for a goodbye?" Tanner asked wryly. He and Lilah had dated all through high school and college before he'd decided it was too claustrophobic for him to stay in Mistletoe, but he couldn't ask her to give up the town she loved. "Been there, done that. Wait, we're not talking about me. You didn't mean just a hypothetical, did you? It would help if I knew more about the details."

"Yeah. I wish I understood those better myself." David looked away, wondering if he should have swallowed his pride before now and asked his parents for their input. Susan had said even they'd had their share of rough patches. As he stared idly down the mall corridor, his gaze caught on a window display of baby furniture. A white wooden crib gleamed in the center, its starkness mediated by the rainbow-colored baby blanket and a cheerful mobile hanging overhead.

He found himself grinning suddenly. Who said he had to wait until next Christmas to start playing Santa to their child? Maybe a present like this would remind

Rachel of all they'd dreamed of together, all they still had in common and could share.

"Tanner, could we part company for a little bit?" They'd been planning to meet the girls at a Mexican restaurant at the other end of the mall in about forty minutes. If David walked fast, he should have enough time to make some purchases and sign some delivery slips.

ALL WEEK Rachel had been tiring out faster than normal, and after a day of walking through stores, she was ready to crash. Even Lilah, caught up in her relentless holiday cheer, noticed Rachel's energy flagging.

Lilah consulted her watch. "We still have a few minutes, but what say we grab a booth at the restaurant a few minutes early and gorge ourselves on chips and *queso?*"

"Yes, please."

They'd worked their way through half a bowl of melted cheese when David arrived, Tanner moments behind him, only one black-and-gold plastic bag between them.

Lilah twirled the straw in her margarita. "You two seemed to have missed the point of today."

"I've actually got most of my Christmas shopping under control," David admitted, sliding in next to Rachel. Her entire body went on high alert at his nearness.

"I made a stop at the car," Tanner said, "to hide my stuff in the trunk. Lilah peeks."

"I do not," she protested.

"You're terrible," he countered. "Alone in a room for twenty seconds with a package, you're shaking it, weighing it, doing everything but x-raying it and you probably only stop short of that because you don't have the right equipment."

"All a legitimate part of the gift-giving experience." She sniffed. "Rachel, David, help me out here. Trying to figure out what's in the box is a time-honored tradition. It's not the same as peeking, is it?"

"You and David must be kindred souls," Rachel said. "He can guess what's inside just by looking at the wrapped package."

David grinned at her. "Not every year."

She knew he was thinking of his birthday a couple of years ago, when Rachel had outwitted him. She'd bought him running shoes he'd insisted cost too much for him to splurge on, then put the box from the store inside a larger box, repeating the process three times until his best guess when he saw it had been a confused "new grill?" even though the one they'd owned was still in good condition. Far more fun had been the small green gift bag she'd weighted with decorative garden rocks one Valentine's Day so that the beribboned package had been appallingly heavy, giving no hint that the real present inside was a gossamer pink-lace chemise she'd worn for him later that evening.

It hadn't stayed on her long.

"You're blushing," David said quietly.

"No, I'm not. My cheeks are just flushed from the spicy salsa."

He laughed.

"You guys gonna tell everyone on this side of the table what's so funny?" Tanner wanted to know.

"Nope," David said. "Private couple stuff. I'm sure the two of you understand, as sickeningly mushy as you are."

"Hey, we've been on our best behavior today," Lilah said, eyes wide. "I haven't called Tanner sweetums a single time."

Next to her, Tanner shuddered. "Whatever you do, don't start now."

"Of course not. You know that's not my idea of romantic conversation." Lilah slid closer to him on the vinyl seat, her voice dropping progressively as she whispered in his ear. "I'm more likely to say something like…"

Tanner cleared his throat, then looked across the table. "You guys eat fast. I have plans after this."

Rachel chuckled along with everyone else, not so much fatigued now as sleepily sated. The food was excellent, and the company was enjoyable. She savored her chicken fajitas while Lilah confessed her top-ten list of things she worried would go wrong at the wedding. They swapped humorous tales of faux pas they'd witnessed, including the ceremony David and Rachel had attended early in their own marriage where the bride's veil had been singed during the lighting of the unity candle—particularly ironic since her groom, the one responsible, was a fireman.

"I remember your wedding," Tanner said, smiling at Rachel and David. "Flawless. The two of you are so organized, so perfect together."

Rachel squirmed in her chair, startled when David took her hand, his fingers caressing hers briefly.

"Rach deserves the credit for that. The ceremony was at her family's church, and she took care of all the details."

"What was it like?" Lilah asked, snuggled against her fiancé's shoulder.

"It was raining that day," Tanner began.

"Which is supposed to be lucky," Rachel interjected, "but I've never understood how people risk having outdoor weddings."

"The storm let up during the ceremony. We all went outside to wait and throw birdseed as they got in their limo." Tanner's face grew more animated as he described the scene for Lilah. "I kid you not, just as they emerged on the church steps, the sun broke through the clouds and a rainbow appeared over their car. You can see it in some of the wedding photos. It was like they were driving off into their own Hollywood ending."

Rachel bit her bottom lip. Hollywood ending? If they weren't careful, it would be more like a tragic independent film with a depressing soundtrack.

"I don't remember the rainbow," David admitted. He was responding to Tanner's story but staring into Rachel's eyes. "I barely remember *anything* about the day, except how beautiful you looked, watching you walk down that aisle toward me and knowing I couldn't possibly deserve you."

The golden boy of Mistletoe not deserve *her*? But his aquamarine eyes radiated so much sincerity she couldn't think straight. "David…"

"I know, I know. I'm giving them a run for their nauseating and mushy title. I should stop." He managed to tear his gaze away, his voice more composed when he glanced at Tanner and Lilah. "If poor Ari were here, she wouldn't be able to keep down her food. Thanks, though."

Tanner raised an eyebrow. "For?"

"Reminding me of that day, how lucky I was. The wedding goes fast. All those months of planning, and then it turns out to be this blur. Try to hang on to it. Keep those memories, and don't ever take each other for granted."

Lilah's gaze was watery. "If you're making me cry now, I can just imagine the damage you'll do during the toast!"

"Wear waterproof mascara," Rachel suggested. "That's my plan." For getting through the ceremony, anyway. She was no longer certain how she was going to make it beyond that. When David said things that were so sweet and devoted, it was hard to remember why she'd ever believed they should be apart.

THE BABY book Rachel had retrieved from the very back of her closet warned that pregnant women were prone to vivid dreams, something to do with estrogen fluctuations and their effect on REM sleep. The book also assured mothers-to-be that in a time as emotional as pregnancy, nightmares were common and shouldn't be taken as omens that something was wrong. Rachel was not having nightmares, though.

Far from it.

Saturday night, after the drive back to Mistletoe in the intimate dark of early evening, her husband's body so close to hers in the cramped backseat that she could feel his heat through her clothes, David had stayed on her mind long after she'd fallen asleep. She'd awakened in the middle of the night from embarrassingly detailed erotic dreams, tangled in sweaty sheets with her body still throbbing in pleasure. Sunday night had brought more of the same, dreams that haunted her thoughts while she got ready for work on Monday. It was difficult to focus on something as mundane as mailing labels when, at random moments, she'd reexperience the slide of David's muscled body against hers.

During the middle of one such flashback that afternoon, she tugged at the collar of her sweater, suddenly feeling as if it was about ten degrees too warm in here. Good thing May had run to the bank with the afternoon deposit, or Rachel would be fielding questions about her clearly flustered state.

She was jarred back to reality by an insistent buzzing, a printer alarm that signaled a jam. Bending her knees, she squatted down to correct the situation. With a little effort, she wrestled the crumpled papers free and hit Continue. The cranky printer claimed the next two sheets as sacrifice, eating them, as well. Swearing softly, she turned the machine off, then back on, waiting for a blinking green light before she tried again. The first page had just printed successfully when she heard the front door open.

"Hello," she called, standing to greet a potential customer. "I'll be right—" Tunnel vision pressed in around her, darkening rapidly to no vision whatsoever as her head went balloon-light and floaty. She thought she managed to squeak out a final word, though she wasn't sure what, before she fell.

When she came to, Rachel was too disoriented to know how much time had passed. She was on the floor by the industrial printers, her feet propped on a carton full of paper. May was fanning her with a spiral notebook, worry pinching her face as she spoke into the phone cradled at her shoulder.

"Oh, you're awake! Thank God. David, she's awake."

Rachel blinked, still dizzy.

"You want something to drink, sweetie? Maybe I should get you a glass of water. Here, you can talk to David."

Rachel didn't feel much like talking to anyone, but she was too dazed to do anything but accept the phone pressed into her hand. "H-hello?"

"You stay right there," David said, his voice taut with concern. "I'm on my way."

Her thoughts began to clear enough for a twinge of humor. He wanted her to stay *exactly* where she was? "You don't have to…"

"Rach, I'm coming over. It's nonnegotiable. See you in a minute."

Then she was left with only a dial tone as May fussed about what to do next. "You probably shouldn't lift your head to drink, but I can't find a straw. Am I supposed to have you breathe into a paper bag?"

That didn't sound right. "I think for fainting, it's supposed to be head between the knees." Although it was probably too late for that in her case. Rachel swallowed, taking stock to see if she was hurt and whether her heart rate was normal. "Really, I think I'm okay."

May continued wringing her hands as Rachel sipped the cool water. "You scared the dickens out of me. I walked in the door, you popped up from behind the counter, then just crashed over like a tree. All that was missing was someone to yell *Timber!* It took ten years off my life when I couldn't get you to answer me."

"Sorry. Was I out long?"

"Nah, just a moment or two. Felt like more when I was panicking. I probably should have called 911, but I dialed David over at the store without thinking."

"No, I'm glad you didn't call 911," Rachel said. As it was, she was already mortified. "I'm fine now."

She was fine. A horrible thought struck her, making her tremble with sick apprehension. Was the baby okay? Falling couldn't be good for the pregnancy. She didn't have long to obsess over that, however, before David burst into the shop.

"Rachel!"

May stood, waving at him. "Back here."

He rounded the counter at top speed, his gaze frantic and his skin ashen.

Rachel was stunned. *He looks worse than I do.* At least, he looked worse than she imagined she did.

Kneeling next to her, he cupped her face in his large hands, his touch infinitely tender. "You okay?"

"Yeah. Just stood up too fast. But—" She broke off, scared to put her fears into words.

"I called Dr. McDermott's office and told them I was bringing you in. She didn't hit her head or anything when she fell, did she?" he asked May.

"Not really, just toppled over." May sent another agitated glance toward her only full-time employee, trying her best to look jovial. "You go with the big guy here and let him pamper you for the rest of the day, okay?"

Rachel braced herself to stand, but David had already slid his arms around her.

"I've got you," he said.

"I can—" She lost her words as he scooped her against him.

Mmm, nice. She was reminded of their wedding night, when he'd carried her over the threshold of their hotel room, kicking the door shut behind him and not stopping until he'd reached the four-poster bed. She thought about pointing out that being pressed against him was not helping her light-headed condition, but by then they'd reached his car, and he had to set her on her unsteady feet to open the door for her.

"I feel very silly about this," she said as she buckled her seat belt.

He didn't look at her. "Silly is when cartoon animals slip on strategically placed banana peels, not when the woman I love passes out cold at work." His tone was so even he could have been introducing himself to a stranger, but his knuckles were white on the steering wheel.

The woman I love? Her mouth went dry. She'd heard him say he loved her hundreds—probably thousands—of times, but at the moment, it seemed liked the most dramatic proclamation ever made. She had no idea how to respond.

Fortunately—and maybe because he wasn't sure how she would answer—he didn't give her a chance. "This is the first time this has happened, right? No other fainting episodes we should let the doc know about?"

"Dizzy a few times, but they always passed after a second."

At the OB's office, he helped her out of the car, his manner solicitous, but his tight grip on her hand crushing. Feeling firsthand how much she'd alarmed him, she managed not to wince. She let him hold on, sensing that he needed it.

A different nurse than the one they'd last seen ushered them back to wait for Dr. McDermott. Unlike his usual charming self, David was terse, never taking his eyes from Rachel even when he spoke to others. After a quick exam, Dr. McDermott declared there was no reason for worry.

"Everything seems fine," she said in her most soothing professional voice. "This isn't uncommon. You've got extra blood going to your uterus and legs now, your circulatory system's got some adjusting to do. Stand slowly, don't lock your knees, stay hydrated. Make sure you're getting plenty of protein so that your blood sugar doesn't get too low. You did the right thing by coming in today, but I don't want you to worry unduly. If it happens again, we'll monitor the situation and maybe run a few tests."

"Thanks." Rachel breathed a sigh of relief. "So I don't have to go on bed rest or anything?"

Lydia chuckled. "No. But it wouldn't hurt for you to take it easy today and keep your feet up."

"Taken care of," David said, finally starting to regain color in his face.

He looked so adamant that Rachel had a sudden vision of him moving all five of Winnie's pets into their house so he could babysit her 'round the clock.

Once they were back in the car, she told him, "Sorry about today. Scaring you like that."

"You don't need to apologize. It's not like you did it

on purpose. Although—" he gave her a wan smile "—I'd appreciate it if you could avoid doing it again. I'm going to take you home, get you settled. Then I'll go by Winnie's, make sure everyone's fed and give the dogs some playtime outside. Hildie's getting great at fetch. She jumps up to catch the ball and rarely misses. But after I've taken care of them, I'll be back to check on you and fix dinner. Any requests?"

"Whatever's easiest."

When they got to the house, he unlocked the door, waiting as she preceded him inside. It could have been any one of a hundred times—them coming back from Sunday lunch at his parents', returning from a soccer game he'd coached, getting home after a town meeting. *Don't forget doctor visits.* They'd come home from lots of different doctors' visits in varying moods—optimistic that they might finally get their baby, frustrated that, after long months, nothing had changed, devastated that the pregnancy had terminated.

"Wow." He looked past her at the coffee table in the living room. Photos, stickers, scissors and construction paper all lay in assorted piles. "Someone's been busy."

"The scrapbook," she reminded him. "You think they know?"

David shrugged. "Nobody's mentioned it to me, but what are the chances? It's impossible to keep a secret here."

"Not impossible," she murmured. She didn't think anyone knew about their separation. Anyone who'd seen the way he cradled her and carried her to the car today probably wouldn't believe her even if she told them.

He swung his gaze from the scrapbooking supplies back to her. "We should get you to bed."

"Typical guy," she teased, wanting to keep his earlier worry at bay. "Only one thing on his mind."

He didn't smile, though. "If I thought there was even the slightest chance you'd let me join you…"

His words skittered along her nerve endings, and she experienced a Technicolor flashback to her dreams of the night before. Thankfully, he was too concerned about her to attempt a seduction, because she seriously doubted she could resist right now.

"Tell you what," he suggested, "why don't you go to the bedroom and change into something comfy? I'll go pour you a drink. What do you feel like? Maybe I can bring you a snack, too."

Rachel thought about it for a minute. "Apples—"

"—and peanut butter, with a glass of milk?" David grinned at her. "Coming right up."

He knew her well, she thought as she changed into pajama bottoms and a faded Henley shirt. And he took good care of her, especially in situations like today's.

Was she an idiot ever to have resented that? So she had a husband who couldn't grasp that there were times she didn't *want* him to ride to her rescue, striding in like some mythological hero with answers on how to solve all her problems—big deal. At least he tried; at least he cared. Even though the crisis today had been brief, during those terrifying moments when she'd worried something might have happened to the baby, she'd thanked God she didn't have to go through it alone.

Pasting pictures of Lilah and Tanner into the

album, she'd thought over and over about what that couple had been through. Tanner had panicked once and left; it had been a huge leap of faith for Lilah to take him back, trusting that he wouldn't hurt her again. Now they looked at each other as if they were the only two people in the world, radiating so much happiness that seeing them was like staring directly into the sun. It would have been understandable if Lilah had refused to give him another chance, but then, think about how much she would have been missing now.

Think about what you're *missing.* Rachel climbed beneath the sheets, her hand smoothing over the side where David had always slept.

He appeared in the doorway of their room carrying a wooden tray. A tart green apple was sliced and slathered with crunchy peanut butter, just the way she liked. A glass of skim milk sat next to the plate.

Her stomach rumbled in anticipation. What with being so busy fainting and causing panic, she'd missed lunch. "Thank you."

He put the tray across her lap, then sat gingerly on the side of the bed. When was the last time they'd been here together? A wry smile touched the corner of her lips as she recalled the sonogram picture. *About ten weeks ago.*

"Anything else you need?" he asked her.

It was such a loaded question that she merely shook her head, not trusting herself to speak. She took a bite of apple just for the extra security.

"All right. I'm going to run to Winnie's for a little while. The cordless phone is right there on the nightstand, and I'll have my cell with me at all times. If you need anything…"

"I know." She licked a spot of peanut butter off her finger. "And I appreciate it."

He watched her eat, so intent that she held a slice toward him.

"Want one?" she asked.

He huffed out an amused sound that was more than a sigh but not fully a laugh. "You and your peanut-butter apples. Sure, why not?" He leaned forward to take the end with his teeth while his hand came up to hold the other half. His breath was warm against her skin.

Rachel shivered.

He straightened immediately, swallowing a bite of apple. "You cold? I can turn up the heat. Or get another blanket out of the closet."

"No, I'm not cold at all. It was just…one of those involuntary muscle things." She washed down the lie with some milk, struggling with the question she wanted to ask. "David? There is one thing."

"Absolutely." He got to his feet, looking relieved to have a task. "You name it."

"Before you go…" She worried at her bottom lip with her teeth, feeling weak for what she was about to ask and hoping it didn't qualify as a selfish mixed signal, but she was still so shaken from earlier. "Before you go, could you maybe just hold me for a minute?"

His expression was comically dumbfounded. Whatever he'd been expecting, that hadn't been it. "All right," he said slowly. "I can do that."

Sitting against the headboard, he scooted over until

he was almost behind her. She moved the tray onto the nightstand and leaned back, reclining against his chest. Breathing in the scent of him, she let her eyes close, sighing when his arms went around her.

She shifted suddenly, realizing how still and quiet he was behind her. "David?"

"Yeah?"

"Just checking."

He smoothed a hand over her head, trailing it to the end of her dark hair. "I'm here, babe. For as long as you need me to be."

Tears pricked her eyes at the sweet poignancy of the moment. This was exactly what she'd needed, although it might have been unfair to ask him for it.

Within minutes, she was unsuccessfully stifling yawns. "You should go," she mumbled. "Once I fall asleep, I'll be a dead weight on top of you."

"There are worse things that could happen." But when she propped herself on her elbows, he obligingly slid free. "I'll lock the door behind me. You just nap. Sweet dreams, Rach."

Her eyes flew open, and she gave a startled laugh.

"Did I say something funny?"

"No. No, it's just that…" She didn't want to explain that, here in their marriage bed, she was haunted by hot dreams of him. Closing her eyes again, she turned onto her side. "When I left for Winnie's, was it hard for you to be here? In our house?"

He stood, not answering for a long moment. "It's hard to be without you no matter where I am."

Chapter Twelve

A houseful of laughing women was the complete opposite of the quiet, complicated intimacy of the night before, when David had returned to cook Rachel chicken and pasta. Tonight's dinner was Chinese takeout. Arianne had ordered enough to feed an entire sorority house.

Since Rachel and David's house was larger than Arianne's garage apartment or either half of Lilah and Quinn's duplex, the women had agreed to meet here for the Bubble Party. At the reception, before the bride and groom's departure, attendants would hand small decorated bottles of bubbles to each guest. The catch was, someone actually had to decorate three hundred clear plastic bottles in the appropriate wedding colors. With Tanner and Lilah both having spent most of their lives in Mistletoe, they'd invited the majority of the town.

Rachel had carefully hidden her scrapbook materials, and the entire bridal party except Vonda (who was hoping to hit a jackpot on a seniors' trip to the Biloxi casinos) gathered at six-thirty. While the glue guns heated up, the women gorged themselves on mu shu pork, beef with broccoli, shrimp lo mein and egg rolls. Afterward, they formed an assembly line in the living room, wedding-themed movies playing in the background for ambiance.

By the time Nia Vardalos and John Corbett had overcome cultural obstacles and meddling family in *My Big Fat Greek Wedding,* one heart-shaped basket was already full of completed bottles of bubbles. Halfway through *Father of the Bride,* Arianne got up to dig out the corkscrew from the back of a kitchen drawer. She'd brought over two bottles of wine from a Georgia vineyard.

"Okay, what can I pour anybody?" she asked, standing at the edge of the living room.

"The white merlot for me," Quinn said.

"Chardonnay, please." Lilah affected a reprimanding scowl. "But when the tiny green bows end up crooked on these bubbles, you're going to have to explain to my wedding guests it's because you plied us with alcohol."

"Fair enough," Arianne said. "What about you, Rach?"

Rachel kept her gaze on the piece of lace in her hand. "I'm good, but thanks."

"You sure?" Arianne persisted. "It's from that family winery in Dahlonega you love."

"Yeah, but I've almost hot-glued my fingers together twice. Friends don't let friends drink and glue. Maybe later." *Like in six and a half months.*

An hour or so later, as Arianne popped a rented copy of *The Wedding Singer* into the DVD player, Quinn stretched and regretfully announced that she didn't think she could stay much longer.

"I have to be at school at seven tomorrow to administer some makeup tests before winter break and the end of the grading period." She shot an apologetic look at the bride. Since the two friends lived in adjoining houses, they'd driven over together. "I hate to cut the evening short."

"Are you kidding? We've already decorated, like, two hundred and eighty bottles." Lilah looked tickled pink by the progress. "You guys are amazing."

"I can stick around and help for a little longer," Arianne volunteered.

Rachel managed not to wince—she'd actually been hoping everyone would go and that she could shuffle off to bed. "That's sweet, but you don't have to. I can easily finish the few that are left tomorrow."

"Okay." Ari agreed readily enough, but stared at her for a moment as if she had more to say. She bided her time, though, until after the other women had left.

Rachel was stacking all the movies by Arianne's purse when her sister-in-law asked from behind her, "So when are you due?"

"What?" Rachel jumped. "How— Why— Why would you…?"

Arianne rolled her eyes, but her grin was a mile wide. "Oh, that was a convincing denial." She suddenly squealed, throwing her arms around Rachel's shoulders. "I am so excited for you!"

Rachel blinked back tears. Even though it hadn't been the plan, it felt pretty amazing to share the news with someone close to her. "Thank you."

"Now go sit your pregnant butt down and tell me everything!"

"Um, other than what you've already surmised, I'm not sure what else there is to know."

"Well, for starters, when are you due?" Arianne repeated. "When did you find out? Did you set up an elaborate romantic scene to tell David, or did you just kind of blurt it out because you were so excited or did he already suspect or—"

"Whoa. One question at a time. We haven't known for very long at all. David was with me when I took the home pregnancy test. We got the results confirmed by the doctor, but we were waiting to tell people. Obviously."

"I don't think that's gonna work out. No offense, but you and David don't have poker faces. When I went to lunch with the two of you the other day, I *knew* something was up. For one thing, whenever one of you thought the other wasn't looking, you were staring at each other."

Rachel felt her face heat. "We were?"

"Oh, yeah. He was in such a great mood, too. But he's also been tense lately. I get it now. He must be really happy but maybe worried about you and the baby all at the same time. Is everything all right?"

"So far. I mean, I've had a few dizzy spells, some nausea. Dr. McDermott assured us all that was normal. And I've been tired."

"We noticed. You were practically falling asleep over your craft scissors, then you refused a glass of one of your favorite wines."

"*We* noticed?"

Arianne bobbed her head. "I asked Lilah and Quinn if they thought you'd been feeling all right lately, and Lilah mentioned that you'd seemed less than a hundred percent shopping the other day. She also said that you asked them to stop the car because you had to go to the bathroom every five minutes. The way David was hovering at the shower and all that food he brought you? I think everyone suspects, but we didn't want to…"

"Get your hopes up?" Rachel asked, knowing that Arianne was treading lightly because of what had happened last time.

"So when are you going to tell the family? You can't wait until the second trimester—everyone will have figured it out by then!"

She made a valid point. Rachel sighed. "I don't know. I'll have to talk it over with David."

Arianne was grinning from ear to ear again. "I am going to be the *coolest* aunt ever. No offense to Lilah or your sister, but come on. This is me we're talking about."

Rachel experienced a twinge of guilt. Even though it hadn't been intentional, she felt bad that one of David's family knew about the baby and he hadn't been part of the announcement. He would have wanted to share in the moment.

"I know you'll be a fantastic aunt. You've always been a fantastic sister-in-law," Rachel said with feeling. "But right now, there's something I need you to do for me as a friend. Well, two things."

"Yes?"

"First, keep it just between us?"

"You got it—it'll be our little secret!"

Yours, mine, David's, Mindy's, May's, Dr. McDermott and her entire staff… Chloe, Quinn and Lilah had probably all figured it out, too.

"Second." Rachel rubbed her eyes. "Any chance I could convince you to clear out of here so that I can drop into an eight-hour coma?"

Arianne laughed. "Deal. I'll call you tomorrow, okay?"

Once Rachel had the house to herself, she brushed her teeth and changed into a silky, oversize sleep shirt that buttoned down the front. In the darkness, she climbed into bed, but her conscience nagged that there was something she should do before she let herself sink into slumber. After only a minute or two of deliberation, she reached for the cordless phone.

Would he be asleep? It was a few minutes past eleven, and David liked to be up with the sun.

He answered on only the second ring, sounding plenty alert. "Rach? Is that you?"

"Hey. Sorry for calling at this hour."

"You can call anytime. Is everything all right?"

"Absolutely. No problems today. But…something happened tonight that you should know about."

"All right." From his end, there came rustling and a click. Rachel imagined him sitting up, turning on the light and bracing himself for whatever news she might have.

"It's nothing bad," she reiterated. "Your sister caught me off guard."

He snorted. "Ari has a way of doing that."

"We were all over here working on party favors for the wedding, and after Quinn and Lilah left, Arianne asked me point-blank about being pregnant. I didn't mean to tell her, but I didn't deny it convincingly."

"You're a very honest person," he said, his voice laced with affection. "So my sister knows?"

"She said she won't tell anyone, but I figured now that the cat's out of the bag, it would only be right to let the rest of your family know. Soon."

"Christmas is right around the corner. Why not tell them Christmas morning?"

She smiled at the idea. "That sounds festive. With the big announcement as backup, I won't have to worry about whether your family will like their presents."

He chuckled. "Oh, come on. They'll love whatever you got them because it was from you."

She picked at the fringe on the edge of her bedspread. Their bedspread. "Actually, I did all right shopping for most of your family, but…"

"But?" he prompted.

"I was at a loss as to what I should get you. Everything seemed either hypocritical or too impersonal." When he didn't say anything, she couldn't help asking, "Didn't you have trouble picking something out for me?"

"No."

"Oh. Well, I—"

"Rachel, it doesn't matter. It's the thought that counts, and I… Really, it doesn't matter." His voice lowered. "There's only one thing I want, anyway. You."

Her breath stuck in her throat, her skin tingling at the intensity in his voice. She was suddenly, miraculously, not the least bit tired. *You,* he'd said—not the baby, not another chance at their marriage, simply *you.*

"I…" Maybe it was a surge of hormones, maybe it was old-fashioned lust, but she couldn't turn away from what she was feeling. Not this time. Didn't she *want* to be that bold woman who went after what she wanted, a woman who wouldn't cower away from making love with the lights blazing?

"Last night?" she prompted. "When you were leaving after dinner, I really wanted you to kiss me. And when we said goodbye after shopping with Tanner and Lilah. And when you picked me up for shopping with Tanner and Lilah. I should have just taken action."

Now she heard *his* breathing hitch as he fumbled for words. It was a delicious sensation.

"Give me five minutes."

PLEASE don't let her change her mind, please don't let her change her mind. David shoved his arms through the sweatshirt he'd discarded earlier and took the steps two at a time toward the front door. Part of him thought it would be quicker just to sprint toward the house—the way he felt now, he could make it in twenty seconds flat—than mess with the car, but then he'd show up sweaty and panting. That was only romantic under certain very specific conditions.

What is it you think is going to happen? he asked himself as he turned the key in the ignition. So she'd admitted to wanting to kiss him. That didn't necessarily translate to...

But instead of listening to what was probably the voice of reason, he focused on thinking positively. He let himself dwell on the way she'd responded when he'd kissed her over a week ago. Such heat. It had to mean she missed him at least a little. And what about the way she'd looked at him during their dinner with Lilah and Tanner, and her request yesterday that he hold her? He couldn't help believing that things between him and Rachel were shifting for the better.

Pulling into the driveway, he barely had the engine shut off before he flung open the door. *Now what, Einstein?* Did he approach this casually, asking if he could come inside so they could talk about what she'd said? Or did he just plant one on her, not giving her the chance to take back her rash admission, and hope for the best?

The porch light was on, probably a holdover from the ladies' visit earlier, but there was no visible illumination from inside the house. He stood in the pale orange glow and rapped against his own front door.

It swung open immediately, his wife smiling up at him from the shadows. "What took you so long?"

A streak of pure need jolted through his body. "Rachel."

That was all he got out before he reached for her, pulling her into his arms where she belonged. His mouth fell on hers, and she kissed him back fervently. She tugged on his hair as if trying to bring him closer. He was happy to oblige.

It wasn't until a gust of particularly frigid December wind hit them that they both realized their front door was standing wide-open. He shoved it closed and turned the dead bolt. The good news was, they'd been in the dark foyer and there were unlikely to be many witnesses at this time of night anyway.

Within seconds, he'd turned back to Rachel, but apparently it had been enough time for her to go. His heart pounded an anxious drumbeat as he struggled to read the situation. Had she suddenly had misgivings, or was she simply awaiting him in their bedroom? As if in response to his questions, a thin ray of light appeared, beckoning him toward the living room.

She was at the sofa, leaning one knee on it without really sitting.

He said the first thing that came to mind. "You're beautiful."

She blessed him with an ageless smile, full of feminine secrets. "I feel beautiful."

Her fingers flirted with the button at the top of her shirt, and David suspected that he would die on the spot. Except that, if he did, he'd never get to make love to Rachel again.

He approached her slowly, curious, not wanting to rush her or take charge of the seduction. As he'd climbed out of his car, he'd been trying to decide on the best plan of action here. Why hadn't it occurred to him that Rachel might have her own plans?

Mesmerized by the slow slide of the button from its buttonhole, he stopped inches from her. A second button followed, revealing the creamy swell of her breasts. He had to touch her.

He rested his thumb over the third. "May I?"

She nodded, her eyes echoing the urgency he felt. His fingers actually shook as he unbuttoned the shirt and parted the satiny folds of material. Her breasts were so full, their centers darker than he remembered. It made him crazy that her body had started changing with pregnancy and he'd already missed some of it.

Recalling what she'd discussed with the doctor, he asked, "Are they too tender?"

She arched toward him. "Only one way to find out, I guess."

Keeping his touch featherlight, he trailed two fingers over the slope of her left breast, slowing so that it took forever to reach the tightly puckered nipple. "That hurt?"

Wordless, Rachel shook her head. He wanted to smile, but his entire body was humming with arousal. Still, he focused his concentration on being gentle, bringing her pleasure. He slid the fabric off her shoulders, glancing down to take in the sight of his wife wearing only a pair of pink panties. For just a moment, he slid his hands down over her rib cage to her waist, then back up to her breasts. When he moved to lay her back on the couch and lavish her with more attention, she frowned, tugging instead at his shirt. He struggled free, glad for the sudden cool air against his skin. It might be December outside, but it was an inferno here.

Rachel placed a palm against his chest and gave him that smile again, the one he felt down to his toes. He sat, helping steady her with his hands as she straddled his lap. The urge to bury himself inside her, to reclaim what was his, was overwhelming. But he hadn't touched her in weeks—hadn't truly explored her in months—and he refused to deny either of them the experience.

Reaching up, he cupped her breasts together, still gentle but merciless in his attention, running his thumbs over the peaks, bringing her close enough to his mouth to suckle. When she cried out, he had to double-check that he hadn't caused her any discomfort.

"No," she assured him. *"More."* Her voice sounded exactly like the woman he'd once thought he knew as well as himself, but also not. It was a dizzying, exotic contrast.

He continued to use his tongue and lips against her

sensitive flesh, and she bucked in his lap. Edging one finger beneath the band of her panties, he found her slick and ready for him. Having been pushed to exquisite, excruciating limits, he yanked down the combined waistbands of his pants and boxers. She braced one hand on the sofa back for balance while she shimmied out of her own underwear and he sat paralyzed, absorbed in the sheer joy of watching her, the warm light of the end-table lamp bathing her lush curves in gold. She looked like a decadent, pagan treasure. His treasure.

Kissing her again, he slid her across his thighs, so close now that all rational thought fractured and flew. Meshing his hands in her hair, he angled her head back, wanting to look into her eyes as he thrust upward and impaled her. For just a second, their gazes were locked together as intimately as their bodies. Then she leaned forward, rocking in a rhythm that quickly doubled and grew frantic. Fingers clutched on slippery skin and half-formed words of carnal praise were traded breathlessly.

She called out his name, one of the few coherent things either of them managed, just as her muscles constricted around him. Feeling like an exile finally home, David tightened his embrace and lost himself inside her.

Chapter Thirteen

They lay together stretched out on the couch for some time, dozing but neither of them falling asleep for long. David idly massaged the small of Rachel's back, which she seemed to like, judging from the occasional sighs.

He kissed the top of her head. "I don't think you told me—what actually tipped Ari off about the baby?"

"A combination of a couple of different things. A biggie seemed to be our lunch with her the other day. She said it was obvious there was something we weren't telling her."

The comment lodged under his skin like a splinter. He and Rachel had definitely been keeping secrets, and not only the happy news of the pregnancy. As for the other? It was probably impolitic to ask where they stood relationship-wise while he still had her naked against him. They'd dragged an afghan over their bodies as their temperatures dropped back to normal, but neither of them had bothered to dress. Just being around Rachel when she was this uninhibited made him want her again.

Would she expect him to stay the night, or would taking a step that gargantuan be overkill? Despite himself, he grinned. After what they'd just shared, it was hard to imagine anything else being seen as too much, too soon. "I hate to leave you, but I guess I should get back to the dogs."

She nodded. "I suppose that's the responsible thing to do."

He felt around for various pieces of clothing while she watched, her expression inscrutable. "Rach, I can't tell you how glad I am that you called."

She shot him a smile so wicked it was probably illegal in fifteen states. "Well, you kept saying that if there was *anything* I needed…"

He laughed out loud, a tremendous weight off his chest. For the first time all year, he felt deep down in his soul that they were going to be okay. It would take work, and it wouldn't happen overnight, but they were going to be okay.

His mother was right—this was the season of miracles.

WHITE ROSES awaited Rachel when she walked into work on Wednesday morning.

May nodded toward them with an approving grin. "Someone loves you."

The words gave Rachel warm fuzzies. All morning, though, the quick pulses of joy were followed by nervousness. When she'd suggested to David in November that they go their separate ways, she'd been almost numb. Even he, by tacit admission and his total lack of protest, had acknowledged how much their relationship had deteriorated. Now… Last night had been like regaining feeling in a frostbitten extremity. Along with the extreme pleasure he'd brought her, he'd awakened a dormant pain. Because, for the first time in a long time, she truly *realized* how much she had to lose.

She made herself wait half an hour, rather than give in to her eager impulse to call him. Instead, she contacted Belle Fulton with some bids she'd put together for the chamber of commerce, then helped May organize a promotional calendar for the coming new year, with seasonally themed discounts and specials. The entire time, David was at the back of her mind, patiently waiting.

Her fingers shook as she dialed the number she knew by heart, and she smiled wryly. Where was the brazen woman who'd slowly stripped for her husband the night before? Had he guessed that when she reached for that first button, part of her had been petrified? It had been so worth it, though. She'd felt glorious, powerful, cherished.

"Waide Supply. David Waide speaking."

"Hey. This is Rachel Waide speaking."

She could feel him smile into the phone. "Hey, gorgeous. I was just thinking about you. Of course, that's because I haven't stopped thinking about you since I left last night."

"Glad to know I made an impression." She glanced around, making sure May was busy and out of earshot, then lowered her voice. "So, I was thinking."

"Go on," he encouraged. "It worked out really well the last time you called me to share your thoughts."

She laughed, but the nervousness that had been dogging her expanded sharply in her lungs—like when you take too deep a breath in really cold air. "David, last night was wonderful, but it might have been a bit…premature. We might have moved a little fast."

"I was really hoping this conversation was going to go differently," he said, forlorn.

"But I liked the direction we were moving in," she added. "I thought maybe we could, um, date for a little while? I know, you probably think it sounds stupid, but—"

"It sounds a whole hell of a lot better than losing you," he said emphatically.

Relief coursed through her. "In that case, I ordered two tickets to the Winter Wonderland Dance. What are you doing Friday night?"

INSTEAD OF falling into the family business, Tanner Waide had struck out on his own. He ran a small but steadily growing bookkeeping service out of his apartment. In fact, despite what Lilah and Tanner conveniently let their parents and guardians believe until after the wedding, David suspected that makeshift office was about the only purpose the apartment served anymore. During work hours, when Lilah was at the school, Tanner could almost always be found here.

David knocked, more relieved than he would have expected when his brother called out, "Just a sec!"

A moment later, the door swung wide. "Dave, hey. Come on in, but watch your step. My lease is up at the end of the month, and it's a maze of boxes in here."

"I see that." The little one-bedroom had never been much to look at, but with so many of Tanner's personal belongings already packed, the place was dingier than usual. Was this Mistletoe's answer to a bachelor pad? He shuddered, wondering how close he'd come to a future that looked like this.

"What's up?" Tanner asked.

David sat on the lumpy orange sofa the landlord had thrown in with the deposit of the first and last month's rent. "I came by to see if you wanted to grab lunch, but maybe it's better if we talk where no friendly neighbors can overhear us. I need to ask your help with something."

"*My* help? Wow, knock me over with a feather."

David raised an eyebrow. "Let me know when you're done making jokes."

"What makes you think I was joking?" Tanner dumped some haphazardly stacked CDs out of a blue milk crate, flipped it over and sat on the plastic cube. "Don't keep me in suspense. What do you need?"

Covert help with furniture assembly, but the simple request didn't spill out.

Instead, David stumbled over the urge to blurt out everything that had happened for the past month and get his brother's relationship advice now that he'd been gifted with a second chance. But, aside from the fact he and Rachel had agreed not to discuss that with his family, David wasn't sure he was even capable of that conversation—admitting that he had made such a hash of his marriage that his wife had left.

Why was this so hard? Everyone—Tanner, Ari, their mother—had made it clear they'd be willing to listen, to provide any kind of support that was in their power. Yet, even with a close-knit family, David didn't make a practice of turning to others for help. By the time he was

in fifth grade, he hadn't needed assistance with home-
work and by the time he'd hit middle school he'd been
earning extra money as a peer tutor. He'd never had his
heart broken as a teenager, had never had to worry about
finding a job and had been blessed with a college scholarship. Even when it came to the kids' soccer teams, he
was one of the coaches able to manage without an assis-
tant when they didn't have volunteers. What his mother
had said to him a few weeks ago was true: *You were the
solution finder.*

Were being the operative word. He was not only be-
ginning to realize there was nothing wrong with occasionally leaning on others, he suspected that if he didn't
start getting comfortable with that idea, he really might
lose Rachel. For good. Besides, he was going to be a
father. While he hoped his kid would grow up to be self-
sufficient, David wanted to set the most positive
example possible—and that didn't include being too
proud to let people who loved him lend a hand.

He waded in slowly. "Things are…awkward with
Rachel. Nothing I can't fix," he hurried to add, mentally
kicking himself for the qualifier. "What I mean is, I think
everything will be fine, but we're in a delicate stage. I
worry that a lot of times, my foot ends up in my mouth."

Tanner laughed. "Been there a time or two myself."

"I want to make damn sure she knows how much I
love her, even if I screw up from time to time. Tanner,
you can keep a secret, right? Even from Lilah."

His brother frowned. "That wouldn't be my first
choice, but for you, yeah."

"Rachel's pregnant." Just saying the words sent

adrenaline through him, exhilaration building. "We're having a baby."

"All *right!*" Tanner came off the crate to clap him on the shoulder. "That is the best news I've heard since Lilah told me she'd marry me. Congratulations, I am so happy for the two of you."

"Thanks. We're thrilled, obviously, but there are a bunch of other emotions under the surface, too."

"I'm sure." Tanner sobered. "You guys have been through so much. Is she worried about…well, you know?"

"Losing the baby? Whether they talk about it or not, I figure all expecting mothers probably are a tiny bit scared of that during their first trimester. Multiply Rachel's 'tiny' by a million. The doctors told her last time that it wasn't uncommon and that an isolated miscarriage didn't automatically increase the chances of another one, but after the previous disappointments… Last week, during one of those awkward conversations I mentioned, she hit me with the out-of-the-blue announcement that I handled the aftermath wrong. That I wasn't there for her in the right way and she felt alone."

Tanner shrugged. "She probably did. No matter how much you love her, that was something she had to suffer through in a way you'll never experience. I guess the best you can do under those circumstances is be patient, be there for her."

"Yeah, it sounds so easy when you *say* it." David shook his head. "We're working to make our relationship really solid and now we have this baby coming! I want to do something for Rachel, a special Christmas present, a grand gesture that takes her breath away and shows her how invested I am in our future as a family. The thing is, it's too big for me to pull off by myself. You're pretty handy with a hammer and power drill, right?"

"I dragged you marathon shopping, and your favor includes the use of power tools?" Tanner grinned. "Man did I get the better deal."

RACHEL KNEW it was irrational to splurge on a dress that would probably only fit for the next forty-eight hours, but she didn't care. While it would still be weeks before people could pass her on the street and tell she was pregnant, her body was definitely changing. Especially her breasts, which had gone up at least a cup size since she'd taken that pregnancy test. The gown she'd chosen for tonight's dance was a shimmering graphite material that crisscrossed over her chest, accented by a slim band of rhinestones and hematite beading, and made the most of her ample cleavage. It fell away from the bodice in a gracefully flowing skirt that didn't cling in any unflattering places. A warm but sophisticated black wrap would keep her from freezing when she was outside.

She'd just finished curling her hair when she heard the doorbell promptly at seven. David looked positively yummy in a blue dress shirt, black blazer and slacks.

"Hi." He smiled down into her eyes, making no attempt to mask the naked hunger in his eyes. "You look stunning."

"Thanks. You, too."

It was silly how much energy adolescents expended on being nervous about dates that included hamburgers and a guy they'd only go out with twice before moving on to the next crush. Tonight, Rachel had a date with the man who—if she was very lucky—she might spend the rest of her life with. She couldn't imagine higher stakes. As a result, she was terrified, especially since she'd previously assumed all of her dating experiences were behind her.

"By the way," he said as he helped drape her wrap over her shoulders, "I'm having something delivered here on Monday. I'll be here to wait for it, if that's okay with you. It's during work hours, so I shouldn't be in your way."

"You have every right to be here. It's your house," she pointed out.

He opened his mouth and she could see that he wanted to correct her: *our* house. She wanted that, too, not just a house, but a loving home for them and their child. Something of that magnitude was worth working for, even if it took a little time and renewed efforts.

Once they were in the car, she asked, "So, with the Wonderland dance being a town tradition, did you take dates there back in school?"

"Sort of."

Intrigued by the hint of laughter in his tone, she waited for more. "Explanation?"

"Well, you know how crowded it always is. I'd go with a girl, we'd make sure to casually bump into her parents and my parents exactly once, then we'd fade into the crush. And spend the rest of the night necking at Mistletoe Cove."

"I'm shocked at you. A boy with your sterling reputation exploiting a charity event for the chance to make out with girls?"

"Don't knock it till you've tried it. In fact…" He slanted a tempting sidelong glance in her direction.

"I don't think so." She wasn't sure she could stop with necking. "*Slowly,* remember? No turbo boosters."

"You sure?" His voice dropped to a cajoling octave. "I'd let you be in the driver's seat."

"I'll bet. As I recall, you quite liked that last time."

His grin flashed in the darkness. "So did you."

Heat zinged through her. David Waide was flirting with her! The sensation was just as heady now as when they'd first met. More so. Then, she'd simply been a woman in her twenties pondering where to go next with her life, and he'd been a very cute guy who'd seemed empathetic. Now, she knew them both better, had seen the promise of how good they *could* be together and had looked into the abyss of how it could all go wrong.

"Rach?"

Her voice came out huskier than usual. "I think we'd better stick to well-populated areas tonight."

"You're undoubtedly right."

But he sounded every bit as depressed about the decision as she was, which cheered her considerably.

FOLLOWING a wonderful date Friday evening—ending in steamy kisses on the doorstep because Rachel hadn't trusted their combined willpower if she invited David in—came a night out with the girls.

Since both Lilah and Tanner had agreed they didn't want to be out partying the night before their wedding, they were holding their bachelor and bachelorette parties the weekend prior to the ceremony. Much to

Lilah's relief, Arianne's talk of a wild and crazy bash had been slightly exaggerated. Still, they did drive toward Atlanta to an upscale club that featured male dancers and really, really cute waiters. One of Lilah and Quinn's colleagues at the school had a minivan that seated eight, so the entire bridal party and three teachers piled in to ride together. Vonda suggested before they left Mistletoe that the women draw straws to pick a designated driver—Rachel drew admiring praise and friends for life when she volunteered.

Once at the nightclub, Vonda suggested they hit the dance floor. "Ever since the hip replacement of '05, I've been a new woman!"

"Okay, but first Lilah has to put on her veil," Arianne insisted. It was a joyfully tacky affair with blinking neon lights and a cellophane-wrapped green condom that looked like an oversize circular jewel in the center of the headband.

A good sport, Lilah slid it on her head to the sounds of her friends laughing and clapping.

Rachel leaned in, keeping her voice to a whisper. "Make sure that thing accidentally falls off on the dance floor, and I'll accidentally trample the heck out of it. Sadly, I'll have to throw it away. Inevitable party casualty."

"Don't tell Ari," Lilah whispered back, "but you are definitely going to be my favorite sister-in-law."

The club was having a retro-themed night, and Rachel had a great time joking with her friends and belting out the lyrics to songs from Abba, Blondie and Barry White, but it didn't quite compare to the night before, dancing to more staid holiday selections in

David's arms. Lilah unknowingly echoed that sentiment later while they stood at the bar and waited for a couple of glasses of cold water.

"Having fun?" Rachel asked.

"A blast. Although having that one dancer come to our table…"

Rachel grinned. "Vonda certainly seemed to like him."

"I think everyone's having fun, and Arianne did a good job planning something naughty without completely destroying my comfort zone. I mean, the dancer was hot, I admit." Lilah fanned herself with one of the small square napkins. "Seriously hot. Still, the only guy I want getting that close to me is Tanner."

"I know exactly what you mean," Rachel assured her. *All I want for Christmas is David.*

Chapter Fourteen

"Have I mentioned how much I appreciate this?" David asked, studying the planks in front of him and matching them with the diagram in the instructions.

On the other side of the room where he was assembling a matching bookshelf, Tanner wiped a sleeve across his sweaty brow. "Happy to help. Although I gotta admit, it's not how I pictured spending my Christmas Eve. I was planning on letting Lilah catch me beneath the mistletoe. A lot."

Both Lilah and Rachel were currently sleeping at Susan and Zachariah's. The Waide tradition was that the whole family gathered there for Christmas Eve and dove into presents first thing in the morning, just as they did when they were kids. Because David had told everyone he shouldn't leave the puppy alone all night, the women were having a slumber party in Arianne's old room and the guys would rejoin them around sunrise. But he'd been serious about not leaving Hildie alone all night— she was camped outside the doorway, gnawing on a chew toy and regarding their progress with friendly curiosity.

David dismissed his brother's lascivious hopes.

"Despite whatever you had in mind, Mom was planning on making sure the two of you slept in separate rooms until after the wedding—"

"Three more days!"

"—so look at this as a way to burn off your physical frustration in the meantime."

"I've long passed physical frustration and am headed into physical exhaustion," his brother groused good-naturedly. "Moving the guest room furniture *into* the garage and all this stuff *out* of the garage… You really think Rachel will be surprised? I'd do anything in the world for Lilah, but she would have found the boxes by now. She has present radar. She stumbles over things I've hidden away even when she's not purposely looking for them. Trying to keep her from finding her engagement ring early was a comedy of errors."

David shook his head. "Rachel rarely ever goes into the garage, especially in the winter." The space was too cramped for them to park cars inside, and had become little more than a storage facility for lawn and mainte-nance tools—it had been the perfect spot to hide the boxes for a few days. Even if Rachel had ventured out for a better look, she would have seen a neatly stacked row of cardboard, all taped up and full of parts and pieces that required assembly.

He grinned at all they'd managed to accomplish in just one night, trying to imagine her face when he showed her. "For future reference, Tanner, I owe you a beer."

"Ha! I was thinking a keg." But his brother was smiling, too. "As long as Rachel loves it, that's enough for me."

David couldn't agree more. This was going to be the best Christmas ever.

RACHEL FELT warm and contentedly cocooned in the dreams she'd been having, but her senses were starting to provide solid motivation for waking up, too. The alluring scent of baking cinnamon rolls, for instance. And she was aware of the gentlest, coaxing pressure... She returned the light kiss as she opened her eyes, waking in David's embrace.

He sat on the bed, smiling. "Merry Christmas."

She sleepily returned the smile, then remembered where she was and glanced around. "Where's everyone else?"

"Arianne's helping Mom with breakfast, which is nearly ready, and I think Tanner dragged Lilah off in search of mistletoe. He was pitiful last night. The way he carried on, you'd think they were separated for weeks on end instead of a few hours."

Rachel stretched, grinning nostalgically. "I remember the days before our wedding when I was sleeping under the same roof as my parents, only I couldn't sleep because I was thinking of you."

"Yeah?" David stroked his hand over her face. "What kind of thoughts?"

"Hey!" Arianne called from the hallway. "If all you happy couples think you're gonna get fed, I demand help in the kitchen."

Pulling herself into a sitting position, Rachel laughed. "Your sister is really going to have to learn to be assertive and ask for what she wants."

"Yeah, well, it's hard, being the baby of the family and a girl," David deadpanned. "Tanner and I probably sheltered her too much. I blame myself for her crippling shyness."

Rachel was still shaking her head and chuckling when she walked away to brush her teeth. She smiled at her own reflection in the mirror. Hard to believe that cheerful, beautiful woman was really her. If anyone had asked her a month ago, she would have said this was her last holiday with the Waide family, probably her last holiday as a Waide. She would have expected it to be tinged with melancholy if not outright grim. She'd never been so thrilled to be so wrong.

The biggest improvement might be her and David trying to reconnect, but it wasn't the only improvement.

In weeks past, she'd been trying to decide if she could be truly happy here, in a slow-paced job and in a small community where people would probably always see her first and foremost as David's wife with no real picture of who she'd been before. But after calling South Carolina last night to wish her own family happy holidays and hearing how stressed they all sounded— Kate having only returned to her job from maternity leave a few months ago and now worried about balancing her career with two small children, Rachel's father still pushing himself as hard as ever and refusing to consider retirement, her mother still obsessing over office politics ("First it was the sexism and having to prove myself among the Boys' Club, now it's making sure these new young girls they hire don't make the rest of us obsolete")... Well, it was easy to remember why Rachel had dropped out of that particular rat race and sought the sanctuary of this sleepy town.

Folks in Mistletoe might be overly interested in her life, but it was by and large legitimate interest, not just judging her by her portfolio or whether she was on track for a promotion. Rachel had never truly disliked her job at the print shop. She'd just started overanalyzing it because she'd wanted to feel that she was in control of something, because she'd so desperately needed to be excited about *something* in her life. But both her parents had tried to find their satisfaction at the office for years, and neither seemed to have succeeded.

She patted her tummy, looking down. "And then there's you." She could not wait to see everyone's faces when she and David made the announcement later.

When she finally joined the others in the kitchen, Tanner harassed her about women taking a long time in the bathroom, and Arianne playfully accused her of ducking breakfast chores. Only David glanced at her with worry, raising an eyebrow in silent question and miming being queasy. It took her a moment to figure out what he was doing, and she laughed at how ridiculous he looked. She'd unintentionally discovered that her competitive husband would probably be lousy at charades.

I'm fine, she mouthed.

To everyone else taking their seats around the table, she said, "Sorry I was late. I stopped and took a few minutes to…count my blessings. A list that definitely included all of you." After a month of her emotions being so close to the surface, she shouldn't be so caught off guard by the way her vision suddenly blurred with unshed tears.

Susan looked startled but touched by the declaration. "What an absolutely lovely thing to say, dear. You know we love you, too. I think it would be appropriate if we all said something we were grateful for this year.

I'll start. I'm the luckiest woman in Mistletoe to have all three of my grown children home and gathered around me for the holidays."

Next to her, Zachariah nodded. "I'm grateful the store had another profitable year and grateful for the work my family put in to help make that happen. David, I haven't once second-guessed turning the reins over to you, and I know you'll do great things."

Tanner kissed Lilah's hand. "I'm thankful this one hasn't come to her senses yet and realized she could do better than me."

A ripple of laughter went around the table, and Lilah's eyes twinkled when she added, "*I'm* grateful the wedding dress still fits—I had my doubts after some of the buffets at Christmas parties we attended. But I officially picked it up yesterday and it was just as perfect as ever. I'm incredibly grateful that, in three more days, I will become Mrs. Lilah Waide."

"I'm grateful I got that waiter's number at the club we took Lilah to," Arianne said smugly. "Well, we don't all have to go for the sap, do we? I figure everyone else has got the cheesy covered."

David's voice was so soft that Rachel wondered if anyone else heard him when he said, "I'm grateful for fresh starts."

Her heart squeezed.

He cleared his throat, setting his hand atop hers on the table. "Rachel, do you want to…?"

Now? She hadn't really thought about when they'd make their announcement, but David was smiling at her eagerly, obviously ready. Why not? Everyone was together, and it did seem like a perfect moment.

She took a deep breath, lacing her fingers with his. "Well, there is one new blessing that I—we—wanted to share with you. David and I are, um…" The tears fell then as if the happiness inside her body was too big to contain and it was seeking any physical outlet. She swiped at the dampness on her cheeks, nearly laughing aloud with sheer joy. She probably looked as if she'd come unhinged. "I'm pregnant! Dr. McDermott says everything looks good so far, and we're expecting a baby this summer."

Squeals and exclamations erupted around the table, and Rachel thought Arianne did a credible job of looking surprised. Chairs creaked as everyone got up to hug everyone else. Zachariah's eyes were misty with emotion when he embraced her. Susan was sobbing hard enough to rival Rachel herself.

After getting her hug, Lilah bounced around the room declaring, "I knew it. I *knew* it! Oh, this is the best news ever. Just think, Ari, by the time you get married, your niece or nephew will probably be old enough to serve as an adorable ring bearer or flower girl."

Arianne snorted. "If I get married, we're eloping to Vegas, but thanks for thinking of me."

RACHEL SNUGGLED against David's side, closing her eyes and listening to the classic movie everyone else was watching. It had been such a wonderful day she didn't want it to end, but she was bone-tired. For as delicious as Susan's roast turkey and white cheddar mashed potatoes had been, they weren't exactly energizing foods. If her body felt this heavy and languid *now,* Rachel couldn't begin to fathom what the third trimester would be like.

"I should get you home." David kissed the top of her head. "You look ready to drop, and I'll bet Winnie's animals would appreciate getting dinner."

Rachel nodded her consent, then exchanged goodbyes with everyone. They'd all be together again the day after tomorrow for the wedding rehearsal and dinner. Tanner had two friends driving up together from Atlanta for the ceremony, but most of the bride's and groom's relatives were local.

Outside, Rachel paused long enough to appreciate the clear night sky and hundreds of stars winking at her as if they were all in on a private joke. "It's beautiful."

David smiled. "You're just stalling because you don't have the energy to walk the rest of the way to the car."

"That obvious?"

He shifted the packages he carried for both of them and put his free arm around her. "Thank you for one of the best Christmases of my life."

She laughed. "Even with the lame presents I got you?" At a desperate loss shopping this year, she'd landed on a boxed set of CDs from a band he liked and a bottle of his favorite cologne, which was practically a gift to her since she loved leaning close and inhaling the scent.

"I had everything I wanted today," he told her as he stashed boxes and gift bags in the trunk.

"Well, thank you for *my* present." She'd been delighted by the digital camera. It was a truly thoughtful gift, with a much higher megapixel count than her last one, a sophisticated zoom function and the ability to take black-and-white or sepia-toned shots. They'd taken a few test shots today, but she was looking forward to reading through the instructions when she was more alert, and really giving it a workout at the rehearsal, wedding and reception. She already had an idea for a set of nostalgic pictures she could do for the chamber of commerce using the sepia option.

David started the car. "Actually, I have one other thing to give you. At the house."

Her lips twitched. "Is that your idea of a come-on line?"

"No." He laughed at her. "I really do have another present waiting for you at the house. Tanner and I set it up last night while you were at Mom and Dad's."

"Oh." That sounded big. She wondered what it could be, but her curiosity wasn't enough to keep her awake.

The motion of the car, the white noise of the engine and the road beneath them lulled her to sleep, but it was only a short ride and she woke a few minutes later, more groggy than refreshed. Would David's feelings be hurt if she asked to postpone unwrapping her second present until tomorrow?

Oh, don't be a killjoy, she chided herself. Christmas came only once a year, and he was obviously excited. She could prop herself up long enough to appreciate whatever it was he'd done for her.

Inside the house, he flipped on the hallway light and turned to her with a huge smile. "This way."

After a second, she realized he was leading her toward the guest room. Intrigued, she hid a yawn behind her hand and followed. What was he up to? He walked through the doorway first, but spun to face her so quickly she almost bumped into him.

"Ta-da!" David spread his arms proudly.

She was so stunned at what she was seeing that it took a moment for reality to register. They were standing in a baby nursery. If it wasn't fully furnished, it was darn close. A white wooden crib, changing table and bookshelf were all assembled and set in place. Brightly colored curtains matched the rainbow comforter and mobile of primary-colored fuzzy shapes.

The world slipped out from under her. Rachel felt as though she were standing on the deck of a ship that was about to capsize; she even reached out for something to anchor herself, but the only thing within grasp was David himself. *All those wonderful possibilities, gone in one fell swoop.* She let her arms fall back to her sides. A familiar feeling was welling in her.

After everything the two of them had been through during the past few months, he still didn't get it.

"Speechless, huh?" He beamed. He moved to the side so she could get a better view of everything. "And here Tanner was worried you might find out, that it wouldn't be a surprise."

"Tanner," she repeated.

David trailed his hand over the crib railing, looking impossibly pleased with himself. "I couldn't have done it without him. At least not under these time constraints."

You shouldn't *have done it without* me. But she bit her tongue, not wanting to lash out, not when they'd been so close…

"So?" He stood there expectantly, waiting for gushing praise. While she struggled to find words, choking on despair, he prompted her as clearly as a drama teacher cuing a nervous student onstage. "It looks great, doesn't it? Works for either a boy or a girl, with all the cheery red, blue, yellow and green. You see we put up a switch plate and that wallpaper border halfway down the wall. If you want, we can paint the trim, too. That might be pretty. Really dresses up the room without painting it all some pastel color we'd have to cover later."

The trim. Her mind was working furiously, one part of her brain pointing out that he'd put a lot of effort into this. He thought he'd done a nice thing. But the rest of her was enraged. She was carrying a baby she'd wanted for the past three years. She'd read parenting magazines cover to cover, thumbed through consumer rating reports and cut out pictures of baby paraphernalia—and David didn't think she'd want any more input on the nursery than what color to *paint the trim?* An aborted scream caught in her throat.

"There's a rocker on back order," he continued, oblivious. "It doesn't match exactly, it's a blond wood, but the cushion will work with what we used in here—"

"By we, I assume you mean you and Tanner?"

He started, seeming perplexed that she wasn't turning cartwheels of joy. "Well…yeah. You're not mad because I told him about the baby a couple of days early, are you? Because I did this for you."

For her, not *with* her. Crucial difference. "I know, David. Th-thank you." Squeezing her eyes shut, she struggled to pull the sentences from her tired brain that would finally make him hear her. She rubbed her temples. "But I had thought that, once we were living together again, *if* we were living together again, we could…that we would— Were you just assuming that everything would revert to the way it used to be after Winnie got home from the cruise?"

"Well, that was definitely my hope," he said carefully. "Come on, Rachel, I love you. You love me. I know you do!" Possibly not the best way for him to argue his case right now, telling her how she felt.

"We're dating right now," she reminded him. "Taking it slowly?" Or had he just been humoring her?

He sighed, shifting his weight. "If it's that important to you, I can get an apartment. Give you your space for a little while. I could stay at Tanner's place if it's really necessary. I'd already decided that if you and I weren't together, you and the baby should take the house, anyway."

Her blood pressure soared. "If you and I didn't stay together, don't you think it should be *my* decision where I lived? You can't make those choices for me, especially not without even consulting me."

"But you already said you'd stay in Mistletoe until at least the birth, maybe longer. It just makes sense for you to stay here," he argued, regarding her as if she were mentally unstable. "Hell, I got this place for you!"

"That's right!" Inwardly, she flinched at her own raised voice, but she couldn't seem to calm herself enough to get her volume back under control. "*For* me, with no input from me whatsoever."

"Well, that would have spoiled the surprise. I knew you'd love this house. And I was right, wasn't I?"

There was no sane way for her to explain that, at the moment, his being right—again—was more a liability than asset. Just as she was at a loss to explain how he could be right and dead wrong at the same time.

"We had been looking for houses on my weekends here," she reminded him, thinking of Lilah and Tanner, building their home, trading opinions on everything from light fixtures to the welcome mat. A surge of envy pierced her. *"Together."*

"But we hadn't found any we loved. This met all your qualifications, and I knew it wouldn't stay on the market long at that asking price!"

All valid points. However, it made it difficult to connect with her husband when, every time she tried to explain her feelings, he cut her off with logical arguments instead of understanding what she was trying to share.

"Rachel, if you didn't like the house, why didn't you say so four years ago?"

If she'd spoken up the moment he proudly handed her the keys—the way she was trying to speak up now—would it have set a different tone for their marriage? "Because I *did* like the house. You were right, of course. It's perfect for us, so it seemed childish to whine, 'But I wanted to help pick it out.' Only now it's four years later, and half the time I feel like a part-time consultant on my own life, with you making unilateral decisions. I wish sometimes that instead of my moving to Mistletoe, where you already had a life established, we'd moved to a neutral location where we could build a life together from the ground up. Because—"

"You love Mistletoe! You always have." He scowled at her, equal parts angry and confused.

Some days more than others. But this wasn't about the town. She was trying to explain her feelings about *them.* "Damn it, David! Could you please just *listen?* I feel…extraneous. I daydreamed about brainstorming nursery themes with you," she blurted, tears rising. "Looking through catalogs, discussing baby names… Unless you've already picked out one of those, too?"

"Don't be ridiculous."

"It's not ridiculous to me, David. I…" She glanced around again, hating how wrong she'd been, feeling stupid for all that hope she'd been nurturing for the past week. "I had this image of the two of us, paint smears on our clothes and faces, standing in the middle of a nursery we'd created together."

"I didn't think the physical exertion and fumes would be good for you and the baby," he muttered, intractable. "I'm sorry you don't like the nursery. I can—"

"No! This isn't about me being some shrew who doesn't appreciate her husband's kind acts. I like surprises. Smaller ones, anyway. This is about *your* entrenched mantra of 'I can.' David, why isn't it ever *we* can?"

She knew she'd ruined the moment he must have been picturing, savoring, while he sweated over furniture assembly and wallpaper paste. She saw the wounded look deep beneath his rapidly cooling gaze and hated herself a little for putting it there…and hated him a little for putting her in this position. This was too important for her to nod politely and pretend she was overjoyed. She'd let lots of incidents pass unremarked— if you could call buying an entire house an "incident"— because they *were* sweet and she didn't want to hurt him. But she couldn't go back to their marriage the way it was. She needed—she deserved—a partnership.

"You make it sound like I don't think about you. I *did* this for you," David protested.

"If you really thought about me, if you really knew me… For a couple of months, I was unsatisfied at my job, partly because I'd fallen into a rut, partly because of the subliminal guilt my parents heap on me that I'm not doing anything more 'important.' I've come to terms with never again having the kind of salary I gave up, never being an executive or having the type of career other people see as important, but I should feel important in my own house. I should feel important to *you.*"

He was furious now, stomping past her as if he couldn't wait to get out of that room. "I was trying to show you how important you are to me! I go out of my way to do things like this, to take care of you, to… And your reactions have varied from sullen acknowledgment to outright criticism. Most women would be thrilled to be married to a guy who thought to send flowers, who surprised them with grand gestures."

"Then maybe I am not the woman for you!" Her pulse was racing, and she couldn't believe she'd just yelled that at him. But this was crucial—the point she was trying to make, this was a deal breaker—and he wasn't hearing her. Again.

David shot her a look of something perilously close to contempt. "Maybe you're not." Then he was gone.

At first she was too stunned to move, but when the front door shut, she sank to the floor, her eyes hot and dry. This felt too big for tears, the gaping hole that had just been punched through her. She didn't know why she was so horribly shocked; after all, she'd known they were standing on a fault line and that one more good-size tremor might be more than their marriage could take at this point.

She just wished she hadn't been so right about them in November and so wrong about them making the most of their second chance.

Chapter Fifteen

David watched his brother through an invisible wall of cynicism. *I don't remember being this discombobulated at my wedding.* Was it because he was a more inherently organized person, or was there something wrong with him? Had he just not loved Rachel as much as Tanner loved his bride?

No, that was ridiculous. *I loved that woman with everything I had in me.* Not that it had been enough for her. He'd told himself for months that the reason he couldn't make her happy was because she so desperately wanted to get pregnant that nothing else could make her happy. Yet here she was, finally pregnant, and still—

"David, I think I left my cuff links in the car!" Tanner said. "I'm supposed to meet Lilah and the photographer in just a sec. Would you mind…?"

"Of course not." David easily caught the keys his brother tossed his way. "Stop messing with your tie, bro. It looks fine. I straightened it myself. And for pity's sake, take a breath."

"Right." Tanner smiled then. "Right, thanks."

See, had that been so hard? He'd given perfectly

sensible advice, which Tanner had recognized and been grateful for. Tanner had not thrown an incomprehensible fit.

A much nobler part of David, which he'd tried to silence at the rehearsal dinner by sipping Scotch and not looking anywhere near his wife, asked, *Is it really that incomprehensible that she wanted to have a hand in decorating the nursery?* But it hadn't just been that. It hadn't only been that after his planning, after his hard work and soliciting Tanner's help, that Rachel had rejected his gift—had practically thrown it back in his face. (How would she have felt if Tanner and Lilah had balked at that scrapbook she'd expended so much effort on? Instead, they'd laughed and cried and hugged her. All the responses he'd envisioned getting from Rachel.) What had chilled David to the core was how easily she'd snapped that maybe she wasn't the right woman for him. It had sounded ominously like a threat. He'd recalled with brutal clarity the shock of when she'd left him in November.

Was that how it would be now, the specter of separation hanging over him like a married man's Sword of Damocles? Would he have to worry that whenever things got rocky at home, calling it quits would be her go-to solution? He couldn't put himself through that. And what about after their child was born? Kids deserved a stable environment.

David's righteous anger lasted from the walk at the back of the church, all the way to the front steps. As he descended toward the parking lot, Zachariah's car stopped at the bottom of the stairs, and Arianne and

Rachel got out. Apparently there had been a hold-up at the hairdresser's earlier. Lilah herself had arrived later than scheduled, her nerves frazzled when she reached the church.

The hairdresser might have been slow, but she'd done an amazing job with Rachel, whose black hair had grown so long in the past year—a result, she'd speculated, of the prenatal vitamins. Now, it was up in some kind of pretty twist, tendrils curling down around her face here and there. Her makeup was smoky and soft, or maybe that was just the pregnancy. He'd noticed the way she was softening more and more lately—well, in general, not with him. Her voice had been hard at the wedding rehearsal. She'd greeted him with exacting politeness, her gaze as warm as an ice sculpture.

He extended that same cool civility now, nodding as she passed. "Rachel." As he averted his gaze, though, trying not to notice how fantastic she looked, it snagged on the top of her dress and the tantalizing view of full, ripe cleavage. That wasn't appropriate for church! But Arianne and Rachel were already hurrying past him and his wordless stupor, leaving him behind.

If it weren't for the fact that he was the best man and took his responsibilities as such very seriously, he would be counting the seconds to the reception and the open bar.

THE GOOD THING about weddings, Rachel thought as she shifted her weight and tried not to look miserable in front of two hundred and eighty guests, was that no one thought anything of it if you cried. She'd wondered, as she first walked down the aisle to her position at the front, whether if she didn't look at David, she could do this. But watching Tanner and Lilah—and the way they watched each other—made everything even worse.

We had that once. They were both good people, flawed but decent, and they'd loved each other very much. How had they let it go so wrong?

Then the vows had started, almost identical to the ones she and David had exchanged. The "richer and poorer" part had never really been an issue, but they'd failed spectacularly at the "better or worse" and "in sickness and health." The promise that really haunted her, though, was "cherish and respect." She recalled mood swings she'd had, excuses she'd made for not being intimate with him, days when she'd been so tempted to roll her eyes at his offering her or someone else advice that she'd forgotten entirely that she used to come to him for advice about everything under the sun.

Had she cherished her husband? She winced guiltily.

David, to give him his due, had tried to cherish her. He'd tried a lot more consistently than she had. But in doing so, time and again he'd failed to respect her opinions, preferences, her intellect and autonomy. Honestly, how much consideration had he really given to why that nursery set would be the one she would want the most, the one that was perfect for their child? Had he simply been swept away by the idea of once again sweeping *her* off her feet? *My husband, the broom.* Of course, as he'd so patronizingly pointed out, lots of other women would be grateful that their husbands cared enough to make sweeping gestures.

Weeks ago, she'd thought miserably that if she had

a chance at taking back small moments in her marriage, she'd do it differently. Was her idea of improvement rejecting something he'd worked hard on, trying to make herself heard at the expense of *his* feelings? God, what a pair they were. Or weren't.

Winnie would be home this week, and Rachel had no idea how she and David would proceed. They had some decisions to make. Unfortunately that would involve speaking to each other again, if they could trust themselves to have a conversation without yelling this time. Maybe that's why some people went to lawyers in the first place, needing that third party. *Lawyers*. Her heart hurt at the thought.

At the sudden sound of applause, she barely kept herself from jumping. Belatedly, she turned to see Tanner and Lilah presented as husband and wife.

She'd missed the end of the wedding, too distraught over the end of her own marriage.

ZACHARIAH, wearing a tuxedo that matched both of his sons', clapped David on the arm. "Should have known you'd be over here."

David jiggled one of the index cards in his hand. "Practicing my speech."

"That's what I mean." Zachariah laughed. "Instead of dancing with that beautiful wife of yours, you're over here trying to make sure it's absolutely perfect. Relax, son, no one's going to grade you on this."

David tried to smile, not quite accomplishing his goal. Luckily his father wasn't looking at him.

The older Waide gestured with his champagne flute

toward the dance floor where Tanner and Lilah only had eyes for each other. "They look so happy together, don't they? As a parent, that's all you can wish for your kids." He smiled back toward David. "I know I wasn't exactly a relaxed or laid-back role model, but when this baby comes, try not to sweat the small stuff. You and Rachel keep loving each other and make sure the little one knows how much he's loved, and the rest will work itself out."

David had always respected his dad's opinion, but that sounded like the most ridiculous thing he'd ever heard. *The rest will work itself out?* Right. Witness his own happy home. Someone should warn Lilah and Tanner how much work marriage took. Then again, under the right circumstances, marriages lasted decades, entire lifetimes. That kind of payoff was worth the effort.

I made an effort.

He glanced across the room, saw his mother and Rachel sitting at a table and talking. From his vantage point, he could see that Rachel had kicked off her high heels and was wiggling her toes. In spite of everything else, the sight made him smile.

He and his wife certainly defined "effort" differently. He thought he'd been making an admirable effort putting together that nursery for her. And *she* thought she'd been making an honest effort to improve their relationship by pointing out why she hated that he'd done it. He frowned. Did she have a point?

It wouldn't make for the wittiest or sexiest reception toast ever, but marriage required compromise. He could tell himself that he'd been working his tail off—trying to pay her more attention, sending her flowers, giving her space while still being persistent in fighting to salvage their marriage—but what had he actually compromised?

The question stumped him. Had Rachel ever asked him to give up anything other than sex on the nights she wasn't in the mood and a few of his more high-handed ways?

Perhaps—that maddening inner voice was back—*if you'd been a little less high-handed, she would have been in the mood a little more.*

"David!" Arianne snapped her fingers, and he blinked, startled to find his sister standing in front of him, a worried look on her face. "Were you even listening to me?"

He was getting that a lot from women these days. "Sorry. What were you saying?"

She pointed to the corner of the room, where tall pieces of white lattice work draped in tulle formed an enclosure around a long table. The wedding cake and groom's cake sat next to each other. "They're going to cut the cake, but first we do our toasts."

"What's yours?"

"That I can't imagine why any woman would willingly live with one of *my* brothers, but that even knowing what pains you and Tanner are, every time I see all that happiness shining from Lilah's face, I get…jealous."

He couldn't believe that was actually her maid-of-honor toast, but knowing Arianne, maybe it was.

"Anyway," she told him, "you go first. If yours is good enough, I'll just add, 'what he said,' and we can get on with the party."

All of the other members of the bridal party were gathered around the table, including Rachel. People naturally shifted so that he could be closer to his wife. Her body brushed his, and his entire system heated with wanting her. He could still clearly remember their own wedding—it had been tormenting all through the ceremony—and how enthusiastically they'd made love throughout their honeymoon. Rachel had lost that enthusiasm in the last year.

Some of that was an understandable side effect of the medications and disappointments, but…was he also to blame? Had David unintentionally made his wife feel unimportant to him, marginalized?

Tanner nudged him with his elbow. "You're up. Bang a glass or something."

David arched an eyebrow. "I've got it under control."

"Good," Tanner whispered back. "I just want everything to be—"

"Perfect?" David remembered his brother saying the same thing to him a few weeks ago as they shot hoops in their parents' driveway. At the time, he'd been tempted to dampen his brother's unrealistic hopes, but maybe those hopes were every bit as realistic as what a person was willing to invest. There were no perfect people, but that didn't mean a man and a woman couldn't be perfect for each other…as long as they worked for it. And, more important, worked *together.*

He held his glass, tapping it lightly with one of the forks he'd grabbed from the cake table. "Hello. I hope you're all having a wonderful time today—" He paused unintentionally, worried about Rachel's emotional state. She couldn't possibly be having a wonderful time. Had she been reliving the same memories as him during the ceremony?

"On behalf of my brother and his beautiful bride, thank you for joining us to celebrate their union." He waited while good-natured applause and hurrahs erupted across the room. Then he glanced at the index card in his hand, and, meeting Rachel's gaze, crumpled the paper.

Her eyebrows rose as he shoved it back in his pocket, but he didn't think anyone else noticed.

"I had a speech all written out, full of brotherly advice about what it takes to make a good marriage, but what do I know?"

Rachel paled, as if he'd suddenly lost his mind and was about to announce to the entire town that his own marriage was a sham.

He gave her a bittersweet smile. "Because the truth is, marriage is a learning process and the very best person to teach you is your partner." *And I'm sorry for all the times I made you feel like less than an equal partner,* he wanted to tell her. It was difficult to keep his voice even. "Tanner and Lilah, you may be surprised at how much you have to learn about each other, stuff you thought you already knew, how even when you think you're getting it right…" What kind of husband was he? Why had it been more important to explain to Rachel why he was right than just to listen to her explanations about the effect his actions were having on her?

For that matter, what kind of brother was he? He'd trailed off in the middle of what was shaping up to be the worst best man's toast of all time.

Rachel stepped forward, suddenly grabbing his hand and smiling. "The beauty of a good relationship is all the new things you'll continue to learn about each other and about yourselves. Celebrate those surprises, celebrate your differences and celebrate the ways you learn to work around them to become an even stronger couple. We wish you many, many years of happiness and lots of love. Cheers!"

Feeling suddenly overwhelmed in front of all those people, including the one who mattered most to him, and as if he were suffocating behind his bow tie, David barely made it through Arianne's quick, irreverent toast and the resulting laughter before he ducked around the corner of the makeshift wall. The back door was only a few steps beyond, and he slipped outside as surreptitiously as possible, feeling guilty for making an escape. He should have at least stayed long enough to thank Rachel for intervening, bringing his mangled monologue to a graceful close.

"Hey," she said quietly from behind him.

Well, here was his chance. Seated on the top concrete stair, he looked over his shoulder. "Thank you for saving my butt in there."

She came closer, joining him on the step but leaving a careful gap between them. "I was afraid you'd be embarrassed that I cut in. Knowing you, you would have regrouped brilliantly all by yourself in another moment or two."

"Brilliantly?" he scoffed. "You must not have been listening."

"Oh, I was." She cocked her head, her gaze almost a

caress. "I…I think I heard what you were trying to say quite well, actually."

"You are definitely the better listener of the two of us." He wanted to reach for her hand but hesitated. "I'm sorry. I'm sorry if it took you yelling or saying goodbye for me to hear you."

Her lower lip trembled, and she bit down on it.

"Rach. Don't cry." He pulled her into a hug, his own eyes damp. "Please don't cry. I'm so sorry."

She glanced up, her eyes round with surprise. "You're crying."

He sniffed, casting about for something to say. "It doesn't count unless the tears actually get out of your eyes. Man rules."

"Ah." She smiled, and the sight of it was like every Christmas present in the world rolled into one. He wanted to be on the receiving end of those smiles for the next hundred years or so.

"I need you," he blurted. "Don't leave me."

Her jaw dropped. *"David."* She launched herself into his arms, pulling him closer and covering his face with kisses.

"That's the most incredible thing you've ever said to me," she whispered.

And then they were kissing each other so fervently that neither of them said anything for a long time after.

When they finally stopped to catch their breath, he promised, "I'll try to do better."

"It's not just you," she told him. "Lord knows there are ways I could be a better wife. You've done so many wonderful things for me, and I should appreciate you more. I should take into consideration the intentions as well as the actions."

"I'll try to stop acting so much without getting your input first. So we'll work on the 'better,'" David resolved. "And consider the 'worse' behind us?"

She nodded, her eyes red-rimmed, tear tracks streaked through her makeup, her professionally arranged hairstyle destroyed by his plunging fingers. She'd never looked more radiant.

"I love you," he told her.

"I love you, too." She wiped her cheeks. "I'm sorry it's not easier."

"Nothing worth having is. And you are definitely worth it, Mrs. Waide."

She blushed, which he found inexplicably arousing. Then again, he'd been aroused since her mouth had touched his.

"Think we should go back inside?" Rachel asked.

"Probably." He grinned at her. "But I'd much rather go somewhere and have my way with you."

She tilted her head up, the sun catching the glint in her gaze as she clucked her tongue at him. "You know, I've heard about boys like you."

"And?"

She traced her index finger over his bottom lip. "And I think you're absolutely perfect for a girl like me."

Smiling in agreement, David kissed his bride.

* * * * *

*Love blooms in Mistletoe in the springtime!
When Chloe Malcolm, mild-mannered Webmistress,
is mistaken for a popular former cheerleader at her
high school reunion, she can't bring herself to tell
Dylan Echols. The former Atlanta Braves player ends
up wooing the wrong—or is she?—woman in
MISTLETOE CINDERELLA,
coming April 2009
only from Harlequin American Romance.*

Here is a sneak preview of
A STONE CREEK CHRISTMAS,
the latest in Linda Lael Miller's acclaimed
McKETTRICK *series.*

A lonely horse brought vet Olivia O'Ballivan to
Tanner Quinn's farm, but it's the rancher's love
that might cause her to stay.

A STONE CREEK CHRISTMAS
Available December 2008
from Silhouette Special Edition

Tanner heard the rig roll in around sunset. Smiling, he wandered to the window. Watched as Olivia O'Ballivan climbed out of her Suburban, flung one defiant glance toward the house and started for the barn, the golden retriever trotting along behind her.

Taking his coat and hat down from the peg next to the back door, he put them on and went outside. He was used to being alone, even liked it, but keeping company with Doc O'Ballivan, bristly though she sometimes was, would provide a welcome diversion.

He gave her time to reach the horse Butterpie's stall, then walked into the barn.

The golden retriever came to greet him, all wagging tail and melting brown eyes, and he bent to stroke her soft, sturdy back. "Hey, there, dog," he said.

Sure enough, Olivia was in the stall, brushing Butterpie down and talking to her in a soft, soothing voice that touched something private inside Tanner and made him want to turn on one heel and beat it back to the house.

He'd be damned if he'd do it, though.

This was *his* ranch, *his* barn. Well-intentioned as she was, *Olivia* was the trespasser here, not him.

"She's still very upset," Olivia told him, without turning to look at him or slowing down with the brush.

Shiloh, always an easy horse to get along with, stood contentedly in his own stall, munching away on the feed Tanner had given him earlier. Butterpie, he noted, hadn't touched her supper as far as he could tell.

"Do you know anything at all about horses, Mr. Quinn?" Olivia asked.

He leaned against the stall door, the way he had the day before, and grinned. He'd practically been raised on horseback; he and Tessa had grown up on their grandmother's farm in the Texas hill country, after their folks divorced and went their separate ways, both of them too busy to bother with a couple of kids. "A few things," he said. "And I mean to call you Olivia, so you might as well return the favor and address me by my first name."

He watched as she took that in, dealt with it, decided on an approach. He'd have to wait and see what that turned out to be, but he didn't mind. It was a pleasure just watching Olivia O'Ballivan grooming a horse.

"All right, *Tanner,*" she said. "This barn is a disgrace. When are you going to have the roof fixed? If it snows again, the hay will get wet and probably mold…"

He chuckled, shifted a little. He'd have a crew out

there the following Monday morning to replace the roof and shore up the walls—he'd made the arrangements over a week before—but he felt no particular compunction to explain that. He was enjoying her ire too much; it made her color rise and her hair fly when she turned her head, and the faster breathing made her perfect breasts go up and down in an enticing rhythm. "What makes you so sure I'm a greenhorn?" he asked mildly, still leaning on the gate.

At last she looked straight at him, but she didn't move from Butterpie's side. "Your hat, your boots—that fancy red truck you drive. I'll bet it's customized."

Tanner grinned. Adjusted his hat. "Are you telling me real cowboys don't drive red trucks?"

"There are lots of trucks around here," she said. "Some of them are red, and some of them are new. And *all* of them are splattered with mud or manure or both."

"Maybe I ought to put in a car wash, then," he teased. "Sounds like there's a market for one. Might be a good investment."

She softened, though not significantly, and spared him a cautious half smile, full of questions she probably wouldn't ask. "There's a good car wash in Indian Rock," she informed him. "People go there. It's only forty miles."

"Oh," he said with just a hint of mockery. "*Only* forty miles. Well, then. Guess I'd better dirty up my truck if I want to be taken seriously in these here parts. Scuff up my boots a bit, too, and maybe stomp on my hat a couple of times."

Her cheeks went a fetching shade of pink. "You are

twisting what I said," she told him, brushing Butterpie again, her touch gentle but sure. "I meant…"

Tanner envied that little horse. Wished he had a furry hide, so he'd need brushing, too.

"You *meant* that I'm not a real cowboy," he said. "And you could be right. I've spent a lot of time on construction sites over the last few years, or in meetings where a hat and boots wouldn't be appropriate. Instead of digging out my old gear, once I decided to take this job, I just bought new."

"I bet you don't even *have* any old gear," she challenged, but she was smiling, albeit cautiously, as though she might withdraw into a disapproving frown at any second.

He took off his hat, extended it to her. "Here," he teased. "Rub that around in the muck until it suits you."

She laughed, and the sound—well, it caused a powerful and wholly unexpected shift inside him. Scared the hell out of him and, paradoxically, made him yearn to hear it again.

* * * * *

*Discover how this rugged rancher's wanderlust
is tamed in time for a merry Christmas, in
A STONE CREEK CHRISTMAS.
In stores December 2008.*

Silhouette®

SPECIAL EDITION™

FROM *NEW YORK TIMES* BESTSELLING AUTHOR

LINDA LAEL MILLER

A STONE CREEK CHRISTMAS

Veterinarian Olivia O'Ballivan finds the animals
in Stone Creek playing Cupid between her and
Tanner Quinn. Even Tanner's daughter, Sophie,
is eager to play matchmaker. With everyone
conspiring against them and the holiday season
fast approaching, Tanner and Olivia may just get
everything they want for Christmas after all!

*Available December 2008
wherever books are sold.*

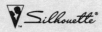

SPECIAL EDITION™

MISTLETOE AND MIRACLES

by *USA TODAY* bestselling author
MARIE FERRARELLA

Child psychologist Trent Marlowe couldn't believe his eyes when Laurel Greer, the woman he'd loved and lost, came to him for help. Now a widow, with a troubled boy who wouldn't speak, Laurel needed a miracle from Trent…and a brief detour under the mistletoe wouldn't hurt, either.

Available in December wherever books are sold.

Visit Silhouette Books at www.eHarlequin.com   SSE24941

HARLEQUIN® Romance®

Marry-Me Christmas

by *USA TODAY* bestselling author

SHIRLEY JUMP

A *Bride* FOR ALL *Seasons*

Ruthless and successful journalist Flynn never mixes business with pleasure. But when he's sent to write a scathing review of Samantha's bakery, her beauty and innocence catches him off guard. Has this small-town girl unlocked the city slicker's heart?

Available December 2008.

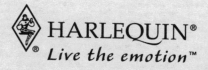

HARLEQUIN®
Live the emotion™

www.eHarlequin.com   HRI7557

REQUEST YOUR FREE BOOKS!
2 FREE NOVELS PLUS 2
FREE GIFTS!

Love, Home & Happiness!

YES! Please send me 2 FREE Harlequin® American Romance® novels and my 2 FREE gifts (gifts are worth about $10). After receiving them, if I don't wish to receive any more books, I can return the shipping statement marked "cancel." If I don't cancel, I will receive 4 brand-new novels every month and be billed just $4.24 per book in the U.S. or $4.99 per book in Canada. That's a savings of close to 15% off the cover price! It's quite a bargain! Shipping and handling is just 25¢ per book, along with any applicable taxes.* I understand that accepting the 2 free books and gifts places me under no obligation to buy anything. I can always return a shipment and cancel at any time. Even if I never buy another book from Harlequin, the two free books and gifts are mine to keep forever.

154 HDN EEZK 354 HDN EEZV

Name	(PLEASE PRINT)	
Address		Apt. #
City	State/Prov.	Zip/Postal Code

Signature (if under 18, a parent or guardian must sign)

Mail to the **Harlequin Reader Service:**
IN U.S.A.: P.O. Box 1867, Buffalo, NY 14240-1867
IN CANADA: P.O. Box 609, Fort Erie, Ontario L2A 5X3

Not valid to current subscribers of Harlequin® American Romance® books.

Want to try two free books from another line?
Call 1-800-873-8635 or visit www.morefreebooks.com.

* Terms and prices subject to change without notice. N.Y. residents add applicable sales tax. Canadian residents will be charged applicable provincial taxes and GST. Offer not valid in Quebec. This offer is limited to one order per household. All orders subject to approval. Credit or debit balances in a customer's account(s) may be offset by any other outstanding balance owed by or to the customer. Please allow 4 to 6 weeks for delivery. Offer available while quantities last.

Your Privacy: Harlequin is committed to protecting your privacy. Our Privacy Policy is available online at www.eHarlequin.com or upon request from the Reader Service. From time to time we make our lists of customers available to reputable third parties who may have a product or service of interest to you. If you would prefer we not share your name and address, please check here. ☐

HAR08R2

Harlequin® Historical
Historical Romantic Adventure!

THE MISTLETOE WAGER

Christine Merrill

Harry Pennyngton, Earl of Anneslea,
is surprised when his estranged wife,
Helena, arrives home for Christmas.
Especially when she's intent on
divorce! A festive house party
is in full swing when the guests
are snowed in, and Harry and
Helena find they are together
under the mistletoe....

*Available December 2008
wherever books are sold.*